Praise for

The Stars and Their Places

"A moving, realistic story of men in combat trying to save lives, and of those at home whom they love. A powerful story of love and bravery."

— David Eubank
Free Burma Rangers

"I loved the book…I truly appreciate wrapping the wives and kids left behind into the story in a fundamental and sympathetic way. My family still bears scar tissue from all of my trips. Good to see that recognized."

— Wm. Brendan Welsh
U.S. Army Special Forces (Retired)

"Vince wrote this book as if he was boots on the ground, observing these events in real-time. The book realistically covers the events near and far that made up Operation Iraqi Freedom in the mid-2000s."

— Landon Chapman
Sergeant USMC, OIF & OEF combat veteran

"A compelling, fresh take on the war novel. Vince Guerra skillfully weaves combat and home front threads though *The Stars and Their Places*. He deals accurately and sensitively with TBI and PTSD, taking care not to fall into easy stigmatizing stereotypes. I was left with one question: When is the next Vince Guerra novel coming out?"

— Clifford A. Brown
Colonel U.S. Army (Retired)

Also by

Vince Guerra

Beyond The Golden Hour

THE STARS

AND

THEIR PLACES

VINCE GUERRA

Edited by Full Spectrum Editing
Cover by Copperlight Wood
Cover background image by Dave Webb
Illustrations by Vincent Guerra V

Cataloging-in-Publication data for this book is available from the Library of Congress.

Printed in the United States of America

Published by Copperlight Wood
PO Box 870697
Wasilla, AK 99687
www.copperlightwood.com

ISBN 9781732571990

Dedicated to those who serve
in shadows and in spotlight,
and to their families,
who are owed more
than can ever be repaid.

CONTENTS

AUTHOR'S NOTE

I vividly recall the day I realized the plot of this book. I was driving to work and pondering the PJ motto *That Others May Live*, and how it might direct someone who can no longer serve in combat due to physical injuries. I always assumed that the word *live* in this context meant to survive death, which it does, but what comes after the rescue? Once the threat of death is lifted, merciless reality comes calling in the form of surgery, physical therapy, hospital bills, wrangling with benefits departments, and a hundred other daily challenges. Added to this is the strain on relationships, personal introspection, uncertainty, and fear of the future. Many survive, but how can we help them to live again when trauma and injury turn their worlds upside down?

As the wars in Afghanistan and Iraq progressed, accounts from veterans became available at an unprecedented rate in U.S. military history. We now have thousands of first-hand accounts from which to draw perspective and inspiration, from every facet of military service, before, during, and after the battles.

As I read them, it became clear that helping veterans regain control of their future was the logical next step for the characters in the previous book. This is a work of fiction. The backdrop upon which these characters interact are real, as are the tools they use, be they medical, military, technological, or even psychological. In my research I strive to achieve as much realism as possible, drawing heavily on memoirs, official reports, documentaries, and personal conversations with veterans to make this fictional world resemble our own.

In spite of my efforts, someone with intimate knowledge of the military will undoubtedly find errors in what I've written. It is my hope that these errors do not detract from the overall message of the story.

Several months into the writing process, I was brought to tears while watching a video of soldiers returning home from deployment, and I felt the weight of what they and their families must have endured. I also knew I could never understand exactly what that was, nor can any of us who haven't walked in their shoes. All we can do is listen to their stories and try to honor them by bringing their sacrifice to light.

We can also say thank you. *The Stars and Their Places* is my attempt at doing that.

PART I

1

Hondo

Tucson, Arizona 2007

I can just sleep now. Forget dinner, forget the shower. Cynthia flopped facedown on her bed. *I don't have to work tomorrow; I can be lazy and not bother.*

Jake isn't here. She immediately sat up, turned on the lamp. Her laptop was on the floor next to the bed, and she reached over and picked it up. She got comfortable and took a sip from her iced tea while it warmed up and downloaded email. A new bold message header accomplished what the scant amount of caffeine couldn't, and now she was wide awake.

Cynthia read her husband's email, savoring every line of its three paragraphs. After the third reading, she hit print; the folded paper would eventually find its place alongside all the others in her top drawer. She glanced at the remaining emails, then set the laptop aside and lay back looking at the ceiling, sick, but not physically. *Three more months.*

The weariness returned and she inched off the bed, shifted her exhausted legs to the floor. She had a little left in her tank and decided she could use a long hot shower. It was always the best place to cry.

Route Michigan, Iraq

The HH-60 Pave Hawk, call sign Hondo Seven, pitched to the right as it passed over the cratered highway littered with the remnant of violent explosions and death. It slowed and made a first pass over the landing zone just off Route Michigan, the main artery out of Baghdad into mysterious places with names like Fallujah and Ramadi — places Americans were growing familiar with, along with terms like *IED*, *insurgent*, and *getting blown up*.

Two Pararescue Jumpers from the search and rescue unit known as Raven looked out the back cabin of the helicopter. Raven PJs like Jake Lyons and his partner Derrick worked in conjunction with their Hondo pilots and crew, two arms of the Air Force Rescue Squadron currently working day and night, ferrying casualties over the battlefields of Iraq.

Tim and Nathan in the cockpit made a wide turn to take in the landing zone. They saw several figures running around waving the Pave Hawk down; none were American.

Jake saw two white junker SUVs, and as the helicopter continued to circle, he saw two Marine Humvees a modest distance from the vehicles. The gunners on each of the Humvees had their top-mounted .50 caliber machine guns aimed at the opposing vehicles.

Hondo Seven continued its sweep. *There it is.*

Several Americans stood around a stretcher, weapons lowered, conversing with five or more men that Jake took for Iraqi militia or police. He didn't know much about what was happening on the ground. Intelligence relayed over the radio en route was only that a Marine vehicle had sustained an IED hit and an American had severe injuries requiring immediate evacuation. It was a standard call; Jake had responded to plenty of them.

The helicopter leveled out into a rapid landing equidistant from the American and the Iraqi vehicles, and the door gunner immediately sighted in on the Iraqis. Jake and his fellow PJ exited on the right and walked around the bird toward the stretcher. The Marines parted for them.

Jake had to shout to be heard over the noise. "What's his status?"

"Hit an IED," replied the officer. "Both legs. Lost a ton of blood."

"Alright, let's get him up."

The Marines picked up the stretcher and moved toward the side door of the helicopter. Jake followed, but before any of them got there he caught movement out of the corner of his eye. Coming around from behind the tail rotor was a man, an Iraqi with a mustache dressed in civilian clothes, speaking words Jake couldn't hear. Jake stopped in his tracks and raised his rifle, sighting in on the man's chest.

"Back off!" Jake shouted as the Marines hoisted their friend into the helicopter, unaware of the man Jake was shouting down. The figure paused, and then continued forward. "Halt! Stop right there!" Jake's trigger finger moved from its rest position. *He's not stopping. You're going to have to shoot him.*

Jake heard .50 caliber fire erupt behind him. One of the Humvees was opening up on one of the SUVs. The thumping sound made Jake instinctively want to turn his head, but training kept his attention on the man in his crosshairs. Jake didn't know what to do. A firefight was starting behind him and this man was just standing there, not holding a weapon, staring...smiling. *What the hell.*

He caught movement out of his left periphery. A massive truck was making a beeline toward the Pave Hawk from the highway. Jake heard the .50 cal hitting it, and thought he saw the helicopter's right-side door gunner opening up as well. The driver was undoubtedly a vapor by now, but it didn't matter. The vehicle's momentum was too great.

Jake was still looking at the smiling man with the mustache. *Oh God.* The world went silent as a wave of heat and light enveloped him. He had the sensation of being lifted from behind by the shoulders under the dominion of some other-worldly force, and still the mustached man was grinning at him, even after the blinding light turned to black, like an imprint one sees with closed eyes after looking at the sun. And then there was nothing.

2

Aiden

Tucson, Arizona

Aiden hopped twice and then dove into the pool, swimming underwater for several body lengths before surfacing. After ten laps, he rested for sixty seconds, and then continued. After twenty more laps, he rested against the wall and looked up at the clock near the rafters. It read 09:25:00.

That's gonna have to do it for today.

Aiden swam casually toward the pool ladder and pulled himself up, hopping up the rungs as he did so, then to the poolside shower. Then he went to a bench where his ball cap, towel, and prosthetic leg rested. Aiden looked around, unscrewed his water bottle, and took a long draft. While guzzling he noticed a young boy a few benches away, staring. Aiden smiled and winked as he recapped the bottle. The boy seemed startled and moved to his mom's side, still staring. She followed his gaze and winced.

"Don't stare, Caleb. I'm so sorry," she said.

"It's alright. How you like the pool?" Aiden asked the young man, who was having a hard time tearing his eyes away from the stump that had once been Aiden's leg.

The boy looked up at his mother as if asking permission, and then looked back. "It's fun." Then he pointed. "Where is your other leg?"

"Caleb." The mom put her hand on her face, mortified. She offered up another weak apology, and Aiden laughed.

"I'm not sure where it is, actually. It didn't work anymore so the doctors gave me this new one. Look," Aiden held up the prosthetic leg for the boy to see, "it goes on like this." He fit it onto the stump below the knee, as the boy watched with wide eyes. When the leg was fastened, he stood up. "See? Pretty cool, huh?"

"Yeah," the boy said. "Can I go swim?" he asked his mother, curiosity exhausted.

"Yes, but we have to go soon." She smiled, and the boy ran back to the water slide. "I'm Shelly," she said to Aiden, extending her hand.

"Aiden. Nice to meet you, Shelly."

"Are you a veteran?" she asked, trying not to stare at his leg.

"Yes. Afghanistan."

There was an awkward pause as they looked at the boy splashing in the pool.

"My husband is in Iraq. Army."

"Oh yeah?" Aiden said turning to face her. "I've got a lot of friends in Iraq. What does your husband do?"

"He's a mechanic. He's in Baghdad, but they move around a lot."

"Has he been deployed long?"

"Over a year," she said looking away.

"Do you guys get to talk much? When I was over there, the links home were pretty lacking, but I hear it's a little better these days."

"Yeah, at least there's that. We Skype pretty often, which is good because every day there's a news story that freaks me out."

"Me, too," Aiden said in a softer voice.

Shelly looked back at the stranger. He gave her the gentle smile of a friend. She smiled back and let out a weak laugh.

"I'm afraid I have to get going," he said. "It was nice meeting you both."

"Likewise, and sorry again about my son's lack of discretion."

"It's really no bother. Believe me, you get used to it." As Aiden walked out he passed Caleb standing in a poolside line for the waterslide. He gave a fist pound to him, and to a few of the other kids in line as he left.

———

Aiden walked into the break room of the clinic and grabbed a paper plate for his blueberry muffin. He was heading for his office when a female colleague stopped him.

"Aiden, did you hear?"

"Good morning, Tami…I'm going to guess, No. Why, what's up?"

"There was an attack in Iraq. A bomb blew up a helicopter, and a bunch of guys on the ground were killed. The news said it was a pararescue helicopter." She looked at the floor, then back at Aiden. "I figured you'd want to know, in case…ya know."

Aiden thought about all the PJs he knew who were currently deployed in Afghanistan and Iraq, as well as the pilots. He was instantly desperate to know names, and which unit was hit. *Hector and Jake are both in Iraq.* "Yeah, thanks for letting me know. I appreciate it."

She nodded and walked off. Aiden went to his office and turned on his computer, forgetting about his muffin, and checked a few news sites but got vague accounts of the event. He decided to call some friends instead to get the unfiltered details, and looked at his watch again. *No time. I'll have to call later.* He got up and went to the lobby.

Aiden turned the corner and saw a young man in his mid-twenties wearing shorts, a t-shirt, and a black ball cap, pretending to be interested in a magazine but primarily looking at his watch. Aiden held out his hand. "Gerry?"

The young man rose to meet him and shook it. "Yeah."

"I'm Aiden. Come on back." He motioned for him to follow, and the man looked around as they entered Aiden's office. The walls were mostly empty except for a clock on one wall and a weathered American flag on another, encased in glass with a placard. The desk held several stacks of books. He glanced at the titles but didn't recognize any. Some looked like textbooks, others looked old, leather-bound, perhaps classics.

Aiden bent down to the mini fridge, pulled out a Mountain Dew, and left the door open. "Help yourself if you'd like something."

The young man looked in the fridge, pulled out a Red Bull, and sat facing the door with his back to the wall. Aiden could tell he was uncomfortable. A signed football on the bookshelf with an Arizona Cardinals logo caught the young man's attention.

"You a Cardinals fan?" he asked.

Aiden smiled. "I guess so. Nowadays, anyway. I grew up more of a hockey guy, but I got to meet some of the players a few seasons ago, so I guess I started rooting for them. You?"

"Nah, I'm Jags," he said.

"You from Florida?" Aiden asked.

"Nah, I'm from Michigan."

Aiden took a drink while the man across from him opened his Red Bull, glanced at Aiden's prosthesis, then looked around, not paying it any mind.

"Thanks again for making time to come in," Aiden began. "I know you probably don't want to be here, hardly anybody does. But there are a bunch of people out there who care about you, and my guess is one of them encouraged you to come here. Am I right?"

"Yeah, my girl. We've been arguing a lot.'"

"Mind me asking what about?"

"Dumb stuff. She says I get annoyed too easy."

"Annoyed with what?"

"Just like, her and her friends taking stupid stuff all serious. She just doesn't get how trivial it is."

"You tried to explain it?"

"Yeah, a little but…how's she gonna get it? So she said, 'Well, then go tell it to someone who does get it.' My corporal said to try it out, couldn't hurt."

"I've seen your intake paperwork, and kinda got a quick rundown on your service record. You had a really long deployment."

"Yeah, they just kept extending it. You got to the point of wondering if you'd ever get home. Now it's like, everything seems different. I'd almost rather be back there."

"You'd probably be surprised how many guys feel the same way. For me it just felt like something was off, and I couldn't tell what it was. Is it like that for you?"

"Yeah, kinda. What happened to you? Over there, I mean?" he asked, pointing to Aiden's leg.

"Got caught up in a bomb blast. Air support, danger close. They ain't kidding. Lived though."

"Sucks, man."

"Right. But I'm alive, and so are you. So the question becomes, what do we do now?"

"I don't know, bro."

"Well, maybe start by seeing if we can identify what seems off."

———

An hour later Aiden was making phone calls to friends around the world, praying he wouldn't be making even harder phone calls tonight. He thought of all the pilots and flight engineers he knew who worked the Pave Hawk, and of all the PJs he had helped train. His main concern was relieved when he finally got through to the Balad Air Base hospital and Hector answered the phone.

"Galindo," Hector said.

"Hector, it's Aiden."

"I hear ya, buddy. I guess you know?"

"Found out a few hours ago. What can you tell me?"

"Bad." The families had not been contacted yet, but Hector knew Aiden would probably be one of the ones holding their hands soon. "Hondo Seven, gone. Derrick, and a bunch of Marines, too. A few are in surgery now."

Aiden didn't know Derrick, but knew he was one of the younger PJs who routinely worked alongside Jake. "Who was the other PJ?"

"Jake. But, Aiden…"

"Yeah?"

"He's alive. Unconscious, a few lacerations, but other than that there's hardly a scratch on him."

3

Hector

Hector looked around at the carnage engulfing him. *I can't stand this place.*

The shattered remains of windows, vehicle parts, and debris of all kinds were mixed with a more horrific variety. Hector couldn't tell what any of the individual pieces had been, but he knew what they were from and it was nauseating. He had never gotten used to it over the course of his career as a PJ, both in Afghanistan and Iraq; he was glad he'd never become callous toward it. It was horror, and as long as he remembered that, Hector hoped he would be able to keep his focus.

He knelt over what had once been a soldier but he had no time to dwell on it. The soldier was dead, but there were others. Hector shuffled over to the next man he saw bleeding. This one was also a mess, but Hector saw hope. The man was conscious and trying to roll over, despite the other soldiers around him trying to help him.

Hector had only stepped off the Pave Hawk a minute ago, but he felt like he'd been here for hours. There were so many missions lately, he hardly had time to think before the next one was on, and every stretch of dirty, sand-covered street looked the same to him now. As his partner put a field dressing on the injured soldier, he saw movement out of the corner of his eye. Before he could follow it to its origin, the soldiers around him started firing at the roof across the street.

The noise of their weapons was deafening and added to their urgency.

"Good to go?" he shouted to the other PJ.

Dave gave a thumbs up. "How's the other guy?" he asked.

"KIA, let's move."

Both PJs picked up the critically wounded man and hurried him through the screen of dust kicked up by the waiting helo's rotor. They moved quickly into the bird and heaved the stretcher onto the floor. The helo lifted immediately and within seconds it tilted away from the landing zone and in a different direction than it came, careful not to pass the same buildings' windows twice.

The wind swirled inside as Hector and Dave assessed how many holes the roadside bomb had made in the soldier in front of them. He was stable, and they'd patched up all the wounds they could find. Fortunately, it was a relatively short hop to the nearest hospital.

He's got a good chance, Hector figured. Then he thought about all of the pieces he'd witnessed on the street. *How many killed? Three, four?* Then he remembered all of the body parts. *No, there were probably a dozen or more.* Maybe not that many Americans, but plenty of dead: civilians, jihadists, kids, poor merchants just trying to live a life in this warzone. The sectarian violence was insane, he thought, as were the attacks on Americans and Iraqi security forces. Death was indiscriminate. It made no sense to him.

The country was a mess, worse than he could have imagined. He often wondered how he would explain this place to Graciella when he finally got a chance to get home. *You can't. Don't try, she wouldn't get it anyway,* he thought.

Hector was no stranger to rundown neighborhoods. He grew up in Laredo, Texas, close to the border. The Mexican gangs had had an informal alliance with the cartels, and Hector had seen his share of violence. He had escaped the gang life, but not all of his family had, and Graci had lost a brother and a cousin when they were younger. Hector joined the military partly to escape. It was a way to get him and his girl safe and make a living, get an education, and raise a big family with a future.

He had three babies at home, but with all his pararescue training and immediate deployments he felt he hardly knew them. He called them his babies, but the oldest, Jasmine, was six. Jasmine's little sisters were four and one.

And here he was, spending every day hovering over half-dead bodies in streets a hundred times more dangerous than the ones he used to cruise as a teenager, while his baby girls grew up without him. Hector ached to see them, and he'd come to believe the worst part of the job wasn't the job itself. He enjoyed the action, saving lives and even occasionally getting into the fight. For Hector, the worst part was the loss – loss of time, loss of people.

Hector tried not to think about all of the men he had lost yesterday. The entire unit was mourning, but with no time to process it the loss turned to anger, and there were missions to focus on. *Derrick, James, Lance, Tim* and…he tried to think of the other pilot's name. *Nathan, I think? And Jake. Thank God for Jake, at least.*

Stop, he told himself. *Just do the job.*

Hector had learned to block it out. He wanted to help everybody, but quickly learned you just do what you can and move on. There was no time to reflect. As soon as they got this guy back, they'd probably have to go out again, maybe to the same street. When they left, there was a small convoy of Humvees and Bradley fighting vehicles pounding away at the building across the street. It was only a matter of time. More would die. *Just do the job.*

Hector and Dave walked the stretcher to the waiting surgical team just inside the tarmac and gave the doctors a quick rundown of the soldier's injuries.

"He's got fragments in his left side, from the ribs all the way down to his legs," Hector said. "Blood pressure is falling, and pulse is weak. He's been unconscious the whole time. Burns all over his back."

"Okay, got it," said the doctor. Then they were gone, into the hospital doors.

Hector and the other PJ retrieved more bandages from a hospital supply cart and got back into the Pave Hawk. The whole transfer had taken less than two minutes.

He wondered if they were going to be heading back to the same street, but soon realized they were returning to their base. He closed his eyes, leaned his head against the wall, and allowed himself to think about how hungry he was, hoping they might be on the ground long enough to grab something to eat.

Soon he was walking into the unit quarters and stowing his gear. He hadn't fired his rifle in a while, but the medical supplies were constantly being used and replenished.

He shut the locker door, stood, and stretched his back with his eyes closed. It was always sore now, the constant crouching and sitting in helicopters taking their toll. He had a clean bill of health but the mileage was catching up with him, and keeping his back in shape was a constant requirement. He knew what it meant to be sidelined on a mission, unable to stand, with lives hanging in the balance. That was the most awful and humiliating day of his life, even though it was no fault of his own – a piece of shrapnel had hit a disk in his spine and he'd fallen like a log. He recovered fast and learned ways of mitigating the pain and the propensity for flare-ups. Still, he was determined it wouldn't happen again.

Hector couldn't remember the last time he had sat down to eat. Yesterday was a wash of activity, none of which included meals. He'd spent most of the day dealing with the loss of the Hondo helicopter and its crew, keeping his men focused, all of whom wanted to go and check on Jake, who was still unconscious when Hector got called out again.

Maybe he's up now, though.

His stomach was growling. He was exhausted and needed calories. *I could eat three sandwiches.* Balad Air Base now had a food court with several American fast food chains and a taste of home was a small comfort, and reliable. But first he wanted to see Jake.

Hector finished putting away his gear and walked to the hospital. When he got to ICU he was expecting to find Jake where he'd left him, but the bed was empty. Hector panicked until he saw Jake walk back to the gurney and sit down on it.

"Hey, Sarge," he said.

"I'm surprised to see you on your feet. Where's the doc?"

"Haven't seen him in a while. Last time he was here, he said I checked out."

"What else did he tell you?" Hector asked.

"I know about the bird, and Derrick. Kai told me."

"Where's he at?"

"Back to work, I guess. He told me to lay back and wait for you, but I had to pee." Jake sat on the edge of his bed and fingered the modest bandage on his forearm. "Can I get out of here? I kinda just want to get back to work."

Hector thought it over, then picked up the charts by Jake's bed. He scanned them, shook his head, and said, "Yeah, let's get out of here. But not to work. Let's get something to eat."

—

Hector finished his first sandwich and opened his second while he looked at Jake sitting across from him. Jake stared into space; he had only taken a couple of bites of his sandwich. Hector looked him over and then settled his gaze on Jake's face.

"Hey Jake, no BS now. I've always been straight with you, right?"

"Roger that," Jake said, looking back and seeing his Master Sergeant looking him in the eye.

"This whole place is a big steaming pile of nasty, but we gotta suck it up. I need to know you're a hundred percent. If not, cool, we'll deal with it. Some guys need more time before they jump back into it, and the Air Force doesn't really give a damn. But us here, we do. You read?"

"Copy, I ain't that guy. I'm good to go."

Hector kept looking into Jake's eyes, and then heard others approaching and he softened. He leaned in close to Jake so the others wouldn't hear.

"Okay Jake, but when you get out there, if something is off, I want you to tell me. Don't worry about the docs. Let me know and we'll deal with it. Cool?"

"Yeah, sure."

They finished their meals in silence. Jake ate a little faster.

"I'll bet Cynthia was relieved to hear from you?"

"I haven't spoken with her."

Hector raised an eyebrow. "Why not?"

"I will, I guess, pretty soon. I just don't really know what to tell her. 'I got blown up, but it's all good'?"

"Is it?" Hector asked.

"You know what I mean," Jake said.

"But she won't. Just tell her you love her, and that you'll see her again soon."

Jake got up, threw away his wrappers, and nodded to Hector as he left.

Hector watched him disappear around the corner. He felt uneasy. There was nothing about Jake that should have given Hector pause to doubt his sincerity or his ability. He was one of the best young PJs under Hector's command, yet he was…he didn't know. He had learned through experience to trust his instincts. When something didn't feel right, that's when people die. Hector couldn't explain it, even to himself, but something about Jake didn't seem right.

What about you. How are you doing? Hector asked himself. He didn't know the answer to that, either. Half a world away, the families of Hector's friends were finding out their husbands and fathers were dead. Graciella would be dealing with that for many days to come. Aiden, too. Hector felt powerless to help the ones he most wanted to – Derrick's widow, Lance's boys…and his own daughters.

He looked at his watch, sat back, and sipped his soda. *We'll deal with that when there's time. Just do the job.*

4

HALOs

Diyala Governorate, Iraq

Something was definitely wrong. The initial jerk of the parachute's deployment felt wrong from the start. The operator beneath began spinning, each rotation more violent. The centrifugal forces became overwhelming and he couldn't establish the terrain, but knew the ground was getting closer. The altimeter on his right wrist was now useless. He needed to cut the primary chute and deploy his backup or he'd be dead in a few seconds.

The lights from the buildings nearby swirled with the inky blackness of the desert, and the effect through his night vision caused a disorientation he'd never experienced. The ground raced up two hundred feet per second, the rest of his team watching from above within their proper descents. He flew past the four who'd jumped before him. The protocol was to follow the lead chute in, but now he was the lead chute and wouldn't manage his landing even if his reserve saved him.

He pulled the cutaway handle and prayed the reserve would open in time to gain some control. The three-ring system detached the main canopy from the container, which then deployed the reserve. It was merciful that he was blind to the ground coming up at him. The reserve chute filled, too late. The rate of fall was slowed but not enough to get oriented, much less maneuver to the drop zone. He tried to establish himself with his legs under his body, but before he could even see his legs he felt the violent snap before he heard it. A sharp pain accompanying a sickening thump in his right ankle knocked him over and he crumpled into a ball. He saw stars, but not in the sky. The pain would wait as training took over and his first thought was of his surroundings.

The green world of night vision revealed the rest of his team descending in perfect formation, a few dozen meters away, off the highway. He pushed his body up off the pavement and looked around, then winced as the bright lights of an approaching vehicle came out of nowhere. He rolled off the highway into the sand, getting further entangled in his chute and gear. The shock, adrenaline, and training tempered the pain he normally would have felt from his ankle, which was now hanging at a ninety-degree angle.

Peetie took a deep breath to try to control his impulses, and reached down. His rifle was not slung where it should be. He looked up at the sky and felt the vibrations from the vehicle on his spine, then heard the tires slowing. He tried to reach for his pistol in his leg holster but it was covered by parachute straps. He tried to think of any way to defend himself, then moved his hand into his vest and pulled out a grenade.

———

A black mass of fabric flapped across the road, then disappeared to the right. The driver pressed on his brakes. He had no idea what he had seen, but he was certain it wasn't supposed to be there.

———

Peetie held the grenade with his right hand and craned his neck to try to see behind him. He knew he could make a lob toss over his shoulder and blow up the truck. *And probably blow myself up with it, and blow the op.* He closed his eyes. They were still inside the vehicle, and wouldn't hear him if he spoke…yet.

He whispered through gritted teeth and heavy breaths. "Arrow One, this is Four, do you copy?"

He inched with slow movements and rolled over onto his belly, felt around for his rifle. He couldn't raise it without cutting the lines of his chute, but he didn't want to move too fast and reveal himself. He saw the doors open and people jump out of the back, and decided to freeze.

"Copy Four, we see you, coming up on your seven. Stay down. Hold your fire," Peetie heard Jenkins say in his earpiece.

Peetie sucked in his breath to stifle the pain that had started up his thigh and into his hip. He put the grenade back in his vest, pulled out his knife, and began slowly cutting the cords around his other thigh.

All six Iraqis were out of the truck and walking toward the side of the road, still unsure of what the driver had seen. They would never know.

———

Jenkins, the assault team leader, thought Peetie was dead when he saw him hit the ground through his night vision, and was relieved to see him roll off the road while he managed his own landing. Jenkins saw the truck, recovered his chute, and hurried to the road. He reacquired visual of Peetie and saw three of the Iraqis carrying rifles as they exited the vehicle. He took a knee to wait for the rest of his team to catch up.

The other three men were immediately behind him. Arrow Two gently squeezed Jenkins' shoulder from behind to let him know they were there, then knelt next to him. Arrow Three did the same.

Jenkins saw the six Iraqis looking into the ditch.

"Take 'em out," he whispered.

Several suppressed shots zinged through the dark, into the bodies of the men who never knew the Americans were there.

Jenkins got to the bodies first and put an extra round into each, just to be sure. Without waiting to be ordered, one of the Americans went to the truck and got behind the wheel, turned off the lights, and drove it off the road while the others dragged the bodies in the same direction. In a manner of minutes the road was clear. Jenkins walked backward scanning for threats and joined the others in the ditch, where his team was already loading the dead bodies into the bed of the truck.

"Eric, you and Tofer drive it off a ways from the road. We'll deal with them later."

"Roger that," Arrow Two said, climbing behind the wheel as Arrow Five got in the passenger seat. They put it in low gear and drove the truck deeper into the desert, and the highway was as quiet and undisturbed as before. Jenkins scanned for threats while he inched backward into the sand, until he crouched over his fallen man, whom Arrow Three, the medic, was assessing.

"Talk to me, Peetie, how bad?" Jim asked.

"Bad. My ankle's done." He swore as he punched the sand. Jim looked over his body, from his head to the ankle. It made an L shape.

"What else?"

"I heard it snap."

"Yeah. Anything else?"

"My hip hurts pretty bad, too. Sorta numb, then pain, back and forth." Peetie was breathing heavily and wincing off and on.

"Alright. We'll get you sorted. Hang tight."

"What we looking at, Jimmy?" Jenkins asked.

"Hard to say. Hopefully just a broken ankle," Jim said

"Alright, let's move him. Fall back to the drop zone."

Jenkins helped Jim slide Peetie onto the collapsible litter. The distance wasn't far but every bounce shook his broken bones. His breathing got heavier and the pain was increasing noticeably. When they reached the truck near the drop zone they got him to a sitting position, and Jim cut away his pant leg.

To the medic's relief the bone was not breaking the skin, though the swelling was severe. It was hard to gauge color in the dark, but Peetie's leg appeared to be discolored all the way up to the thigh.

Intact blood supply to the foot? What else might be fractured? Joint damage, spinal fractures? He hit the ground hard, something else must be broken. He might be bleeding internally. The pelvic pain and numbness could indicate that and also possibly nerve damage, Jim thought. *No way to tell without x-rays. Either way he needs a surgeon, and out of here.*

"Well?" Jenkins asked.

"He needs evac. Could be internal stuff."

"Alright," Jenkins said, then keyed his radio. "Atlas, this is Arrow One, do you copy?"

High overhead, a small single prop aircraft slowly circled the desert. The U-28A waited, listening, for Arrow's call.

"Copy Arrow, this is Atlas."

The new aircraft was a military version of a civilian Pilatus PC-12, but equipped to ferry up to nine passengers onto remote landing strips or provide aerial reconnaissance and communications. In a pinch, it could land on anything passing for an airstrip, anywhere in the world, which made it a sexy addition to the special ops arsenal.

"We have a man down, severe ankle break. He's stable but needs an evac. Please advise."

"Copy that, Arrow. Stand by."

—

Lieutenant Jenkins looked at the highway and felt they were far enough away from it that nobody would notice them unless they had night vision, which some of the Iranian, Saudi, and other foreign troops flooding over from the Iranian border now had.

He looked toward the lights of the buildings nearby. This was becoming one of the most dangerous places on earth, a region swelling with weapons, bomb materials, insurgents, and recruits; they were waiting, planning, regrouping, and rearming after partially fleeing from Baghdad, where the Army was overwhelming them.

The Surge was working. Americans coated large areas of the city, stationed in pockets that the Iraqis saw pop up overnight, beginning to regain the control they'd lost in 2003-2004. Dozens of outposts were manned where Americans were establishing forward operations and taking the offensive, as well as mixing with and befriending the civilian population exhausted by the sectarian violence that had turned their country into hell. Iraqi citizens were stepping up and many were training with American Special Forces, learning how to clear the rats from their ranks.

The insurgents retreated outside the city to lick their wounds and coordinate. And they adapted quickly. Like sharks to chum in the water, jihadists from all points of the globe came and established weapons caches in remote areas near arteries into Baghdad. The town Jenkins was looking at was one of many places intel pointed to as a possible staging area. Arrow hoped to find them within the buildings half a mile away.

Two Apache attack helicopters were waiting to destroy whatever they were asked to, but first Arrow had to get there and verify the target. The war had become increasingly visible; cameras and war correspondents were everywhere. A rocket attack on a building had to be confirmed, and Arrow needed to get in and verify the target. Now they were down a man. Very soon the sun would start to rise. The clock was ticking.

The pilot and copilot were busy in the cockpit of their HC-130, going through pre-flight procedures, feeding information into the aircraft's five menu screens on the top of the control panel. To the right of them, the navigator entered information into another computer on the wall in front of his sitting position.

Outside, the engines hummed and ground crew walked in and around the aircraft. The two engines closest to the fuselage were already spinning, and the two outer ones began to turn and pick up speed. The ground crew communicated visually through the lower windows near the pilot's knees to let him know that all looked well.

Hector moved up the back ramp alongside Jake and two other PJs, Kai and Jeremy, hauling their medical and combat gear. The back ramp closed as soon as they were in and the plane started to move. The PJs settled into their seats but didn't bother getting comfortable; very soon they would be jumping off the same ramp. The lights inside went completely out once they were airborne. They were on their way to a remote circle of desert in northern Iraq.

A few minutes later, the pilot spoke to the PJs over the aircraft's internal communications system. "Have you determined a jump altitude?"

Hector and Kai went over the numbers with pencils in the dark. There was significant wind over the drop zone, and the higher they jumped, the harder it would be for the navigator to put them on target. It would be a risky jump under ideal circumstances, and these were anything but ideal.

They were jumping to recover a special operations team member within an already underway operation, in close proximity to unknown and heavily armed enemies. That meant a low, static line jump was out. It would be a HALO jump, or High Altitude, Low Opening. They would jump in excess of 30,000 feet and open their chutes as close to 1000 feet as possible, factoring in the wind. The lower the opening, the better the maneuverability. They had plenty of desert to play with if they were blown off course, but nobody had time to spend on the ground searching the desert for a wounded man and his team. Kai had determined – and Hector agreed – they would need to jump above 30,000 feet and deploy right at the ceiling. This would allow time to visually identify Arrow's infrared strobe and the surrounding terrain in order to hopefully land right on top of them, unless the wind decided to have its say. It had already claimed one man tonight.

Kai relayed the altitude to the pilot and they felt the plane ascend. The PJs started preparing their gear, and in the cockpit, the navigator fed his information into the system computer in order to get them over the target. The surface winds were steady. The aircrew was sending the PJs out in 22-knot winds, which was slightly over the safe wind speed for their chutes. A civilian jump would never allow it, but these were PJs, and JSOC – Joint Special Operations Command – was not scrapping missions for two-knot wind variances.

The pilot could call it off if he determined it was too dangerous, and the pilot had done this a few times in his career. The aircrew and the PJs knew each other and established a level of trust in each other's expertise; the pilot cared for the PJs' safety every bit as much as his own crew's and wouldn't drop them just anywhere. Hector trusted his judgment, and the relationship between the two teams was what made long term success in a changing war. For this reason, Hector didn't worry about the jump or about what they'd encounter on the ground. He only worried about his men.

Hector looked at Jake in the darkened cabin. Jake stared back, betraying no emotion.

———

Jenkins never heard the HC-130 overhead, but he knew it was there. The Arrow team huddled around their injured member and directed the incoming jumpers, letting out an infrared strobe that the PJs could see as they descended. Despite the wind varying from strong gusts to relative calm, the four chutes seemed to descend perfectly in a stair-step pattern. Two of the Arrow operators kept their eyes on the highway while the other two prepared to link up with the PJs. The first jumper's feet passed ten feet over their heads and landed perfectly, quickly followed by the other three. They were on the ground.

Jenkins watched with his night vision as the four PJs recovered their chutes and walked over.

"Thanks for coming. Nice descent," he offered.

"Anytime. Where's your guy?" Hector asked.

Jenkins turned sideways so they could see Peetie on the ground. "Right here."

Hector motioned for Jake and Kai to take a look at him. It only took a few minutes for the PJs to come to the same conclusion as Jim.

"Needs a surgeon, but we have time," Jake said.

Hector turned his attention to Kai. "Call it in. See what they want to do."

"Copy that."

Hector and Jenkins listened as Kai radioed in the situation on the ground: one man injured but stable and in no immediate medical danger. There were undoubtedly several commanders trying to decide how best to handle the extraction without scrapping Arrow's mission. Waiting for their orders didn't take long.

"Atlas to Arrow. Proceed to target. Raven will assist. Do you copy?"

"Copy that," Jenkins replied, and turned to Hector. "I guess you're coming with us."

"Roger that. Where to?"

"That larger building is our primary target. When we get close, we'll breech the side facing us. Two of you cover the courtyard and surrounding lots," Jenkins said to the PJs, and then turned to Peetie. "You get to sit this one out."

Hector addressed Kai and Jeremy. "You two sit tight with him and be ready to move. Jake is with me."

"Let's move," Jenkins said.

The six men began moving across the dark sand, careful not to kick up rocks, and scanning from left to right with their night vision. In minutes they were within a stone's throw of the building and hadn't seen anyone, just a few mangy dogs scampering across the dilapidated lots. When they came to the wall separating the building's lot from the outer desert, they gathered against and it called a halt.

Jenkins keyed his mic. "Arrow in position. Pegasus, do you copy?"

———

Several miles away, the pair of AH-64 Apaches flew low across the dark expanse. They were in the air as Arrow landed, but had to divert and wait for the mission to get back on track before being allowed to commit. Their fuel was more than sufficient. The real danger was ground fire.

More than a few Apaches had been cut to shreds by highly organized and creative Iraqi ground defences, and although the Apache could take a beating, every minute in the air increased their likelihood of enemy contact. The squadron of Apaches known as Pegasus was used to it by now. Their primary mission was to hunt down and kill enemy targets, and they were on the prowl tonight.

"Copy Arrow, this is Pegasus Eight. Coming up on your target. ETA five minutes. Standing by," a female voice said across the radio.

Genevieve Cooper flew as close to the ground as caution allowed, but if it were up to her, she'd fly lower and faster.

"Looks like we're gonna blow up some buildings to-night," she said to her front-seater, using a mock hillbilly accent. She flew the helicopter from the rear of the tandem cockpit, while Craig Allen controlled the impressive weapons systems.

"Damn right," Craig agreed.

Craig and Ginger had flown together since 2004. After nonstop training and hundreds of missions they had learned the complex choreography of the Apache's crew. They each had control of the 30mm chain gun that would likely be their primary weapon tonight.

Craig used long-range cameras to search the buildings and shadows for potential threats, assessing the proper countermeasures for whatever they might see. Tonight it was all out in the open.

He saw Arrow and the truck with its several dead bodies as indicated by their lack of a heat signature, as well as movement in and around the buildings.

Their aircraft had mounted rocket pods which, depending on the mission, could carry up to 16 Hellfire anti-tank missiles, 76 Hydra general purpose rockets, or some combination of the two. With the combined firepower of Pegasus Six alongside them, they could potentially level the entire city. At the very least, one target building would be hit. It was almost too easy.

———

Jenkins moved at a crouch along the courtyard wall till he came to a break. He was first in line and looked around the edge to confirm the courtyard was empty, then doubled back to Hector and Jake.

"Cover the courtyard from here while we move to the building," he said.

"Copy that," said Hector and Jake in succession.

The four Arrow operators covered the distance from the wall to the back door of the long, single-story building.

———

Jake watched them through the scope of his rifle, panning to the right, up toward the roof, back to the edge of the building. To his left, he knew Hector was doing the same. He looked back at the door the men were about to breach. The Arrow operator tried the doorknob first, just in case.

Nope, Jake thought, as the door stayed fast. They would have to breech it.

One of the operators pulled out a small explosive charge and began the dangerous act of sticking the det cord, primer, and explosive on the door. It was an art; too much and the explosion would ruin the element of surprise. Arrow had no idea what was on the other side of the door, but the operator had it ready in seconds.

Jake heard on the radio, "Stand clear. Ready in three, two, one."

The charge went off and the door blew inward. The four operators disappeared into the building before anyone inside could have time to react.

—

Jenkins secured the corners and blind spots while the men behind him filed through the opening. The room was clear, so they moved farther down a corridor.

Before they got to the next door, a man in a long white robe stepped into view holding an AK-47. Eric killed him before he turned the corner. They moved fast to close the gap, and in the next room they found four men scrambling for weapons stacked along two walls. Jenkins dropped two, but the others got off a spray of bullets before dying, hitting Jim in the left forearm. They kept moving to the next room. Lights were on down the hallway, and they heard female voices screaming in Arabic.

—

"Arrow, this is Pegasus Eight. I have your building. Multiple individuals moving inside to the northeast and spilling outside." Through the thermal imaging on the Apache Ginger could clearly see four men with rocket tubes she assumed were RPGs. They also carried rifles and were attempting to double back around the outside of the building.

"Light 'em up, Craiger," she told her front-seater.

"Oh, I'm on 'em," Craig said. He had already selected his 30mm chain gun from the weapons profile and was targeting the group. He let loose a short burst, turning the four shadowlike figures on his black and white screen into an explosive flash. All movement stopped.

"Let's find some more targets," she said. "Pegasus Six, do you see anyone on the street?"

In the other Apache, Tim Miller had an eye on everything else while Pegasus Eight attacked the building.

"Negative. You've got two friendlies by the wall to the south. Pretty quiet on the street for now."

"Well, that'll probably change in a minute," Craig said from the seat in front of her.

"I know, right?" she said. "Come on out and play, guys."

———

Jake watched four men spill into the street and was about to fire on them when he heard the cannon from somewhere behind him go off, and the group of men disappeared within the green flash of his night vision. He turned his attention back to the breeched door, scanned the roof, and listened, waiting for whatever was going to happen next.

———

Inside the building, Jenkins took a knee and fired three shots into a man down the hall. The wailing voices coming from the room to his right were frantic and loud.

He inched toward the door, turning his rifle into it as he passed, and saw a room full of children and two women in long robes. Jenkins motioned for Topher to take charge of securing the room with the women, and then moved down the hall with his remaining two shooters, one of whom bled considerably from his disfigured left forearm.

Jenkins came to a halt at the end of the hallway and was greeted by bullets coming through the thin walls. He and Eric returned fire through the wall and moved to the edge of the door frame. It was quiet for a second. Jenkins saw blood dripping off Jim's arm onto the debris-littered ground.

"Raven One and Two, get in here, we've got a man wounded. Arrow Five, how we looking back there?"

Topher had his hands full with a room full of screaming, flailing women and crying children. He had to yell several times to get them to sit.

"I could use some help in here," he answered.

"Copy Arrow Five, we're coming up behind you now," Hector said. He and Jake moved into the blown doorway and quickly scanned the room, then turned right and moved toward Topher standing just inside the door and yelling. Jake came up behind him. Topher, with his left hand aiming his rifle, used his right to motion Jake inside. He never took his eyes off the crowd. Hector moved past to find Jenkins.

Jake looked at the women on their knees, facing him but still waving their arms around. He then panned over the children, seven of them, ranging in ages from toddler to about twelve years old, Jake figured; there were no military-aged men. He focused on herding the kids all into the same corner.

"Hey, sweetie, it'll be alright. Go to your mama over there," he pointed and gestured using as soothing a voice as he could manage. "Come on, it's alright. Go to your *um*," which he thought meant "mom" in Arabic. The little girl wiped her eyes and one of the women said something to her, coaxing her over to the others. Jake turned to the two remaining kids, both boys.

The older boy was sitting behind the younger one, who was crying. The older boy stared right at Jake, displaying no emotion. *Is he scared? Frozen by shock?* Jake couldn't tell.

Jake pointed to the human huddle and said firmly, "Move now!" The boy stared back and then looked to a pile of blankets. Jake felt a chill.

Oh God. Jake reached to pull up the rifle that was hanging by his shoulder harness.

Topher yelled from behind Jake, "Kid, get over there now!" But the older boy just sat there behind the younger boy, who Jake now saw was being held in place by the older one. Jake pulled up his rifle and met the boy's eyes. His cross hairs were on the older boy's face, all that was visible from behind his preschool human shield.

"Let go of him and get over there!" Jake took a step toward the boys. The older boy shoved his companion forward toward Jake. The little boy fell while the older one darted for the pile of blankets. Jake recognized the butt of the AK-47 as the boy reached for it and tried to pull it around.

Jake wanted to disarm him but the boy lunged, turning as he fell backwards, trying to point the rifle at Jake. Jake fired three shots into the young man's body, which crumpled in a heap.

The women erupted; wailing pierced the air.

Jake inched forward and examined the young man whose life he just ended. He wanted to drop to his knees and wail himself. He wanted to pick up the boy and carry him away somewhere. He wanted to ask his mother for forgiveness. He wanted to be anywhere else in the world, but instead he keyed his mic and simply said, "Clear."

———

Hector moved through the hallway, glancing into each room as he passed. Weapons and bomb-making materials were everywhere. He came up behind the team at the end of the hall and noticed one of them trailing blood.

The room was empty of enemies — they had escaped the room only to be cut down by the Apache — but seven large banquet-style tables lined the walls, crowded with a variety of canisters, cell phones, wires, watermelons…and explosives. Jenkins was looking out the exterior door that was swung open. There was movement in the buildings nearby, and they heard voices.

"Arrow One to Pegasus, we've got company emerging from the buildings on the northeast corner."

"Copy that, Arrow. We see them, too," she said.

"How's that arm, Jimmy?" Jenkins asked.

"Good to go," he said, before looking down and seeing it was bleeding profusely.

Hector took hold of his arm and applied a bandage to the plug the hole, then wrapped it tight. "Can you grip with it?" Hector asked.

"Not really, deal with it later," Jim said.

Then they heard Jake's shot ring out behind them.

———

"Arrow, be advised we're tracking multiple targets converging on your location. Recommend you exit from the south entrance. Clear for now. We'll sweep the perimeter," the Apache pilot said. Then she spoke to her gunner. "Who's first?"

As she said the words, a series of pings started hitting the helicopter. She pulled hard to the left and spun around at the same time, "Oh, hell no. Did that foolish man just shoot his tiny little gun at my aircraft?" she said, incredulous.

"Sure seems like it," Craig said.

"How dare you, sir. Craiger, tell him what we think of that."

"He can wait. I'll take those guys with the RPG's on the right first." Craig let loose with his cannon again.

"Pegasus Eight. I've got valid targets on the rooftop of the building on the immediate west. Engaging," the other Apache said. Its front-seater got to work, and the results were the same. Targets kept popping up as the Apaches circled, moved horizontally, or hovered just long enough for the bird to take out a target, never sitting still long enough for an enemy to aim at them.

"Craig, you see that truck?" she asked.

"I see everything," he said in his best Schwarzenegger impersonation.

The truck, with at least three men in the back, sped between buildings and stopped in a dust cloud behind a wall. The men stood up and tried to level their weapons at the other moving Apache. Pegasus Six's front-seater already had the wall targeted on his computer and was getting ready to select a weapon when he saw it explode. Craig's rocket got there first.

"Thanks, Eight," he said.

Pegasus Eight was covering every direction on the grid, maneuvering all over the sky. Every time she held still, Craig fired on another target. They popped up in almost every direction, and just as fast, the two Apaches knocked them down. Her main concerns were accidentally clipping into Tim's Apache with their seemingly erratic flying and of running out of ammunition. If this didn't end fast they might need to call in more birds.

"Arrow, this town is waking up pretty quick. Suggest you get a move on," the aviator said as she pivoted at a 45-degree angle and moved to engage two men who were running to the target building.

———

Jake and the other operator had compassion for the women wailing over the dead child, but no time. The other children cried uncontrollably. Topher let his rifle hang and pulled the women off the dead boy, flex-cuffing their hands behind them and letting them fall to the floor. Hector turned the corner and looked into the room, followed by Jenkins and the other team members.

"What the hell?" Jenkins asked.

"Kid went for a rifle." It was all Topher had to say.

"Either of you speak Arabic?" Jenkins asked.

"Negative," Hector said.

Jenkins tried his best to communicate with the mother. "Lady, get up. We're going now." He pointed at the floor, and motioned to the walls and waved his arms around. "Boom. All this. Boom. You understand. Let's go," he repeated several times. The women seemed to understand and started yelling at the children. They got up with their hands cuffed and herded the children out, spitting at the Americans as they moved past, uttering a mixture of foreign curses and grief.

Hector looked at Jake. He had a look Hector hadn't seen before; he couldn't tell if it was anger or something else.

"Jake, let's go," he said.

Jake's attention snapped as out of a daydream. "Good to go," he said out of habit, and moved past Hector. They followed the line of men down the long corridor back to the entrance they had started through.

Once outside, the women and children scattered into the shadows of another courtyard. Jenkins heard the female voice over his radio. "Arrow, you've got quite a party down there. Is the target building clear?"

"Copy that, Pegasus. We're clear. She's all yours," said Jenkins. Last out the door, he trailed his men across the courtyard back to the broken wall.

"Move it, back to DZ. Raven Three, we're heading to you. How's he doing?"

"Arrow One, we see you. All here," Kai said.

"Atlas, ready for extraction," Jenkins said.

—

"Okay Craig, take it out," the aviator ordered her front seater. The Apache let loose with a barrage of Hellfire missiles into the building.

The rockets exploded and caused the rooms full of ammunition and bomb materials to ignite in a chain reaction that created a fireball reaching high into the sky; secondary explosions rocked the buildings around it. People scrambled outside in the streets and through open windows.

"Pegasus Six, target destroyed."

"Copy that, Eight," the other pilot replied.

The Apaches made wide circles in opposite directions, keeping an eye on the burning town and the small group of men moving away from it simultaneously.

—

When Jenkin's team reunited with the men who had stayed behind, he called in again. "Atlas, this is Arrow One standing by. Where do you want us?"

He then addressed his injured man, "How you feeling, Peetie?"

"Pissed off," he said, "Can we get the hell out of here now?"

"Sounds normal to me. Wouldn't be himself if he were ever in a good mood," Jim said.

"You're supposed to shoot them, not the other way around, Jimmy," he teased, pointing at Jim's arm.

"It's nothing, bro. Learn how to use a parachute."

Peetie gave him the finger.

The fixed wing aircraft had been privy to all the action, circling high above and waiting for anything. The pilot thought he could land on the hard sand, but preferred a surer surface. "Arrow One, how's that little stretch of highway look from your angle?" he asked.

Jenkins surveyed the distance from their location. "All clear for now."

"Atlas, this is Pegasus Eight, be advised we're tracking vehicles with armed men heading in that direction from the south."

"Copy Pegasus, can you clear an DZ for me on that road?"

"Copy that Atlas. Stand by," she said. "Pegasus Six, how about you close that road from the north and I'll block it off from the south?"

"Copy, Eight. I've got two vehicles leaving the town, headed that way now," Miller said. "Looks like they're armed. Engaging."

The Apache tracked the speeding cars and headed them off, turning above the highway to point toward them. Tim Miller knew the drivers were looking to salvage the night's utter defeat by killing the helicopters with the RPG tubes hanging out their side doors. A slight smile formed on his lips as he decided to appear to give the cars what they wanted. He dropped to the deck and hovered a foot above the pavement, facing the oncoming cars.

Pegasus Six's front-seater fired off a Hellfire that obliterated the first car, which became a flaming roadblock that the rear car smashed into. A couple of survivors were visible on infrared, crawling away from the second wreck, but after a few feet they stopped moving.

"Road is closed from the north, Atlas. Should be clear, unless they find a bulldozer," Miller said.

"How's it look on your end, Oh Eight?" the Atlas pilot asked.

"Clear and quiet, Atlas," she said.

"Roger that."

—

Atlas needed about 3000 feet to land, and it had that and more along the highway protected by the Apaches. The surveillance cameras on the aircraft never stopped monitoring the wounded man and his protectors, and it would land as close to the Americans as possible. It flew higher and turned over the desert to begin a rapid descent.

"Atlas, I've got three vehicles moving in your direction from the south."

"Craig, I'm gonna get in their face a little," she said as she turned abruptly, dropped altitude, and flew toward the three vehicles moving at their top speed. She wanted to close the distance and splash them as far away as possible to give the aircraft a longer runway to take off.

"Armed?" she asked, meaning the vehicles. They might be non-combatants. It could be someone who saw the fireball coming to help, even though it was more than likely someone drawn to the fight for the opposite reason. Still, she had to identify them before she could fire. There were rules and she abided by them, even if the enemy didn't.

"Can't say," Craig said.

"Then put a crater in front of 'em."

"Copy that," Craig said, and sent a rocket into the pavement ahead of the first vehicle. "Give the Iraqi DOT something to do tomorrow."

The procession stopped with screeching tires as rubble landed on their hoods and windshields.

Pegasus Eight hovered. "Your move," she said, assuming a British accent.

After a minute, Craig saw an object emerge from one of the windows, then a streak jumped out.

"RPG," he called out.

"Naughty boy," she said as she maneuvered her Apache, pitching to the left as the rocket flew past the helicopter. She leveled out, dropped altitude, and began moving sideways all in the blink of an eye. Before the men in the truck could even see where she went, a series of rockets bore down on them as Craig added three more kills to the night.

The burning vehicles made bookend fires on either side of the U-28. The light made Jenkins nervous, but he also had two Apaches circling overhead.

Jake held the end of the stretcher and moved at a trot toward the road. The U-28 was on the ground and the men ran to catch up to it as it came to a rolling stop. The side door opened and the foldout staircase lowered. Two men took up defensive postures in front of the aircraft, whose single propeller never stopped moving.

When they reached it, Jake and Kai pulled Peetie off the stretcher and carried him up the stairs, careful not to jostle his fractured leg. The interior could accommodate a handful of men at most, and Jake began to do a mental head count. Men piled in around him and he wondered if they might have to shed gear to save weight. Hector pushed up next to Jake and the bodies kept getting closer and tighter. Somehow all nine men squeezed into the plane, and it was rolling long before the stairs were closed up and secured.

In the cockpit the pilot struggled to calculate the new weight. The plane gained speed, and the pilot let out a breath of relief when the wheels lifted free. He had control and gained altitude.

When they didn't crash after ten minutes, Jake allowed himself to relax, leaning his head back to look around at the collection of dark and dirty masses. Hector's face was less than a foot away from him and their eyes met.

Hector rolled his eyes, gave a brief smile, and then wiped his forehead. He considered asking Jake about what happened in the room but figured it could wait. It was too loud anyway, and he didn't really want to talk. Still, he felt the prompting in his gut, and the worry.

"How you doing?" he asked Jake over the engine noise.

Jake looked away and saw the face of the boy in his mind. The image was gone as soon as it had come and he shook it off. He looked around at the men again, at Kai and Denny, then slowly back to Hector.

"Good to go."

The Apaches watched from above as the small plane gained speed. It wasn't long before the U-28 was airborne and off, and the Apaches waited to make sure it was out of danger before increasing altitude. The front-seater from Pegasus Six had one more shot to take. He fired a rocket at the truck that was sitting in the desert, which was now abandoned with a bed full of dead Iraqis, their weapons, and extraneous gear Arrow and Raven had left behind.

"Nice shooting, Six. Anything else you feel like blowing up tonight?" she asked.

"Negative. I think we're all done here," Miller replied. "Nice flying, by the way."

"Thanks, old man," she said. "Craig, I feel like singing. Do you feel like singing?"

"Not really."

She started anyway. "Ooooh, show me the way to go home. I'm tired and I want to go to bed..." and as she flew, she swayed from side to side.

From the front seat, Craig joined her. "I had a little drink about an hour ago, and it's gone right to my head."

From behind them, Tim Miller smiled. As the Apaches traversed the dark desert on their way home, he started humming along with them.

PART II

5

McCoys

Tucson, Arizona

Evan McCoy let out a deep breath. He centered the crosshairs of the rifle's scope on the small orange circle of the paper target and pulled the trigger. The recoil that startled him on his first shot was comforting now, and he smiled. This was fantastic. He almost didn't care about hitting the target; he just wanted to fire another round, but his great-grandpa was next to him with a pair of binoculars.

"That's a nice shot, son. A little off the right though. You need to go slower."

"Yeah, sorry. Can I take a few more?"

"That's what we're here for."

Evan looked over his shoulder past his great-grandpa. Behind them, Aiden and Grandpa talked among themselves. Evan raised his voice a little and said to them, "Maybe Uncle Aiden will let me shoot his next?"

"No," all three men said in unison.

"Lame," Evan said, turning his attention back to the rifle in his hands and the target in front of him. Then he felt his great-granddaddy's gaze boring a hole into his neck.

Evan looked up. "Sorry."

"Uh-huh," he grunted.

—

Aiden and his father went back to their conversation.

"So, since you never mentioned her again, I'm guessing things never went anywhere with…was it, Terry?"

"I think you mean Tina, and no. I had, like, one date with her, Dad."

"Well, I don't mean to be up in your business, but your mom was asking so I told her I'd pry a little."

"Right." Aiden laughed. His father laughed, too. "It's not like you're hurting for grandkids, you know. Josey's got four now, Alyse has what, six?" Aiden wasn't sure.

"Yeah, I know. Adopt a few and all of sudden she shoots right to the top of the leader board. It's making Christmas a little tricky this year. So is coming down here," his father said. "Ever think about moving back home? Plenty of vets around. A lot of guys you know."

Aiden looked past the shooting range his grandpa had set up, out into the open Arizona desert. "I don't know. It's pretty beautiful here."

"It's also ridiculously hot. Why your grandpa likes to spend half the year in the desert is beyond me. It's plenty beautiful at home."

"It's a different kind of beautiful," Aiden said. "But Abby's grateful for him being here. Josey's kids need it."

"I suppose they need you more," Aiden's father said.

"I don't know about that. Abby's twice as tough as Josey."

"That's true," his father said. "But moms can only teach them so much. My dad can teach these boys how to shoot and hunt just about anything, but until Josey gets back they need you for the tough stuff."

Aiden looked away. "Maybe."

"They admire you. I admire you. I admire how you give so much of yourself to these guys you're helping now. Back in my day when those guys came back home, some of them were messed up, and then spit on, too. It pissed me off. I'm proud of you, Aiden. These boys see it, and they're sponging it up. Josey knows it."

Aiden looked back at his dad. "You know it was actually sorta easier getting shot at. At least then the enemy was something you could see. Some of the guys I talk to, they just can't see the demons. Simple stuff that a person wouldn't think anything of becomes a threat." He looked away again. "Kinda breaks your heart."

Aiden's dad looked back at him for a long time. "Well, that's another reason to make sure you're taking care of yourself. Go out and have some fun. Lord knows there'll always be brokenhearted people around to help when you get back to work on Monday."

"Yes, sir. I shall have fun. Copy that."

"Punk," his father said.

"He has a point. When was the last time you had a date?" Abigail asked her brother-in-law while they put lunch together. Abigail and Josey's toddler sat at the barstool, helping himself to a bowl of tortilla chips.

"I don't date."

"I know. You might start trying," Abigail said. "And stop whining, it doesn't suit you."

"How am I whining? The constant prying is just annoying, and you of all people know how that can be," Aiden said.

"They just want to see you happy."

"I'm happy."

"Yeah, but they only get to see you what, once a year or so?"

"Well, you can give them periodic updates on my happiness quotient. You were always tattling to my mom anyway."

"You were a jerk," she said flat out.

"How?" Aiden asked, handing a slice of cheese to his littlest nephew.

"Ah, excuse me!? Remember taking a handful of daddy long legs and putting them down my raincoat?"

"Pssh, I was like six."

"You almost died at six," she smiled. "But I suppose you did save my husband's life once."

"Way more times than that."

"Well, true. And in any case, I need you to kill the snakes and scorpions around this place."

They went back to chopping vegetables. Abigail asked, "Are you excited Hector's returning this week? I'll bet he's happy. Perfect timing for football season."

"Yeah, I got him two tickets in case he wants to go to the game I'm taking the boys to."

"You don't think he'll want to? Isn't Hector, like, a superfan?"

"Coming back can be rough. You never know."

Abigail knew. Her husband normally flew high above the front lines, and an A-10 pilot could spend his entire career never seeing an enemy eye to eye. Josiah never experienced it until the day he got shot down high in the Hindu Kush mountains and endured the hell of ground combat, and the weeks of nightmares that accompanied it. But now he was back in the air of Afghanistan, and Abigail prayed he would stay that way.

"Well, the boys are excited anyway."

"Stacy change her mind?"

"No," Abigail said with a hint of sadness.

"She's not really a football fan, anyway."

"Neither are the boys really, but I think it just makes her miss her dad."

"Right," Aiden agreed. Seeing Josiah off to war for his most recent deployment had broken everyone, but none more than his five-year-old. Watching her break down as he left was the hardest thing Abigail ever had endured. Aiden, too. And Aiden had endured plenty.

Aiden looked out the window to the barbecue grill, loaded with burgers and dogs. Grandpa McCoy had a spatula in one hand and a massive water gun in the other, and children took turns trying to climb onto the deck to tag the old man, but getting soaked in the process before retreating.

"You know she's going to be sad she missed it."

"I know. Maybe she'll change her mind." Abigail started to tear up.

Aiden saw it and interrupted her. "Oh, none of that. Come on. Mom and Dad are leaving for home tomorrow night and if they see us crying here, they're going to change their tickets to next week or something. And neither of us wants that now, do we?"

"Oh, no. You're right." She smiled a fake grin. "Happy faces, happy faces."

6

Lyons

Davis-Monthan Air Force Base, Tucson, Arizona

Cynthia strained to see around the huge "Welcome Home" signs and get a glimpse of the C-17 on approach. The sun, radiating on the tarmac, was almost unbearable even to an Arizona native wearing flip flops and the sundress that was her husband's favorite. Cynthia inched around a sign, trying not to be rude to the young boy holding it while sitting on his mother's shoulders. Neither of them seemed to notice her; everyone was focused on the aircraft coming closer and preparing to land.

Until she was twenty-five years old, Cynthia McMillan had never been outside of Arizona. "And why would I?" she once told Jake. She grew up in Flagstaff and loved every minute of it; she never wanted to live anywhere else. She was content with the simple beauty of her hometown, and the vastness afforded by the surrounding desert was candy to an adventurous young girl. When college rolled around she entertained several options out of state, but nothing appealed. She almost didn't bother with it at all, but her parents convinced her the academic scholarship would be foolish to waste.

So she stayed close to home and became a Sun Devil like a few of her classmates. After college she got a job at a bookstore in Tucson to be near her sister, but she never cared much for big cities.

Cynthia was athletic, but not an athlete. She occasionally submitted to her sister who liked to run 10Ks with her friends. But Cynthia had never run another race after she had met Jake a little over a year ago.

—

Why in the world would anyone choose to run six miles for fun? Jake had wondered that morning.

For Jake, running was a means to an end; nothing more. From the first mile he was forced to run in gym class through the thousands he tacked on in high school sports, he hated running. It was the one drawback that almost turned the tide when he debated joining the military.

So he watched the parade of civilians in front of him with equal measures of fascination and disgust. Men and women of all ages and every demographic passed his viewing area, huffing and puffing as they ran, or smiling and chatting if they walked, and Jake tried not to mock them as he sipped his coffee alongside Kai.

They were only there to watch some of the guys from their unit running with their families, lured by the promise of a barbecue later in the day. It was interesting at first, seeing the progression of hardcore runners like Aiden who went past them early, to the novices, and eventually to what Jake and Kai were calling the Stroller Brigade. He was aggressively bored after the first twenty minutes and began looking at his watch, paying little attention to the runners until he noticed a group of three women – one pushing a stroller, saying something that had the other two women laughing. The talker held no interest for Jake. The one on her right, however, had him staring like an idiot.

She smiled and laughed as if she didn't care who heard, and as she got closer, Jake saw an empty ring finger. It was fortunate for Jake the women were oblivious to his presence and didn't see the creepy guy with the sunglasses staring as they passed, or Cynthia's sister Naomi might have ended him then and there.

Jake hesitated at first, thinking maybe he'd see the mystery girl again after the race, then got nervous that she might disappear. He watched her from behind as she began to fade into the crowd. Jake handed Kai his coffee cup. "Hold this."

"Why?" Kai asked. But Jake was already several feet away.

Jake half-turned and smiled at Kai while walking sideways, then tripped over himself and the curb as he tried to keep pace with the group of women who had decided to run the final leg.

Jake got up and moved as fast as the crowded sidewalk would allow, dodging cars and onlookers, weaving around strollers and trying not to knock over street vendors. It was an urban obstacle course and he fell several times. By the time he reached the finish line, he was a sweaty mess and he'd lost sight of the girl behind the banners and balloons. Kicking himself, he brushed off his elbow and started walking toward the finisher's area. He saw Aiden, who appeared to be giving an interview. Then he spotted her.

She was in a group of five women now, clustered together and laughing as they drank from water bottles. For a moment he thought about backing out, but Jake never quit anything and he had come this far already. Jake looked at his muddy, grass-stained jeans and noticed he was bleeding slightly from a scratch on his forearm.

Great. Nice first impression. He tried to give a nonchalant sniff to his underarm but figured it was pointless. He sucked in a couple of deep breaths to regain his composure, wiped the sweat from his forehead, and walked toward her.

Cynthia's sister noticed Jake's approach before anyone else did, and almost laughed at him. As threatening as he may have been in different circumstances, the smear of dirt on his forehead made him look comical. He was obviously in shape and clearly a military guy, but the dirt streak cancelled out his impressive physique. "He was nerdy cute," she would later say.

As Jake approached the edge of their circle, he realized he had no idea what to say. There had been no time to think about it. He smiled, and felt like an idiot. They smiled back, wondering if he was.

Naomi spoke first. "Are you here to take our coffee orders?" The five friends all laughed.

"Hi," Jake said, laughing at himself.

"Hi back," Naomi said louder.

Think of something charming, quick, he thought. He was embarrassed but he had already committed to the mission. He was bold by nature and it took over.

"Ladies, my name is Jake. I'm a complete stranger, but I'm not a weirdo, and I would be happy to buy you all coffee if this lovely lady," he extended an upturned palm toward Cynthia, "would be so kind as to tell me her name."

"Her name is Bambi, and I'll take a hazelnut latte," Naomi said.

"Soy mocha. Thanks," another chimed in.

Now they were all laughing, even Cynthia, who was starting to blush.

"Please forgive my friends." She smacked her sister's shoulder. "Actually, my name is Cynthia. If you're serious, I'll take a sixteen-ounce latte, but first you need to tell us why you have mud streaked across your forehead."

Jake instinctively wiped his forehead again, and then looked at his dirty hand. He made a puppy-dog look and offered, "Um, I had to fight off a pack of ninjas who were chasing after you?"

"Oh really? Tell us more," one of the women said.

"They're all gone now. You're safe. But, I owe you all coffee. If you want to wait here, I can go grab some and come back," said Jake.

"Excuse us while we confer." The women formed a huddle and gestured to Jake to take a step back.

"By all means," Jake said, and complied.

The conference lasted less than a minute while they peeked at Jake and smiled. When they broke, Cynthia and Naomi went up to Jake.

"Sir, I will be happy to meet you for coffee this afternoon at four o'clock." She handed him a piece of paper with a location and her first name, but no phone number. "Perhaps then you can better explain the manner of your unkempt appearance. Good day." Cynthia turned on her heel, her friends did likewise, and they walked away.

I guess "unkempt" means I look like a sloppy idiot, Jake thought.

Five months after their first coffee date, which extended well into the night, Cynthia Lyons was on her first road trip out of Arizona on a camping honeymoon with an Air Force PJ whom her parents adored. A month after that, he was in Iraq.

—

Jake paced around rows of pallets within the cargo hold of the C-17. The long flight home was actually a series of smaller flights and this was the last. Most on board slept through them, aided considerably by sleeping pills, which made medics and PJs the most popular passengers. From Iraq to Kuwait, on to Germany, then to New York and finally, the last leg to Arizona, Jake rotated from anxious, to exhausted, to bored. They waited in hangars, slept on any surface not in the sun, and tried to pass the time on various forms of in-flight entertainment they were lucky enough to have brought home as personal gear, like books, or movies they'd already seen a hundred times over the deployment.

Jake had slept for much of it, but the drug-induced stupor had worn off hours ago, and the makeshift pallet bed he was delighted to stake a claim on over Europe felt like a bad idea now. He watched some of the older guys rocking like babies in their privately purchased hammocks, and made a mental note to buy one for next time. He longed for a breath of fresh air. He was almost home.

Technically, he already was. The aircraft started its descent, and the range of emotions on board was proportional to the number of its occupants. Men who hadn't seen families for half a year or more were wrestling with it all. Some were chomping at the bit to see them; some of the single guys had no one and would end up weaving their way through the throngs of tear-filled reunions as quickly as possible. That was Jake's first experience, and it was awkward. On every previous deployment he had been single and excited just to get off the plane to be home. Jake had been on the combat merry-go-round for years.

Once, his parents had been there to welcome him back; another time, nobody. The last time he had come home, his enthusiasm had evaporated almost as soon as he stepped off the ramp. He hadn't realized how much he had longed for connection, and since he had nobody but his unit brothers — most of whom were busy connecting with loved ones — he had slunk away and driven home alone. That loneliness wasn't a part of life in combat; there was no time for that. Boredom, sure, but not loneliness. At least, not for Jake.

Overseas, he was always working and learning. Jake thrived on challenges and they were a constant on deployment. He had sought them out all his life. He was smart, but more than that, he was daring. Some types debate for hours whether something can be done, but Jake was the one who would simply walk up and try it. He wasn't reckless or stupid; he had a healthy degree of fear, just not enough to make him timid. In fact, few people had ever intimidated him.

He was a natural leader and rarely quit anything. His parents taught him to push himself if he wanted to get better, and he grew up hearing the lesson that he could always excel among his peers or those younger than him, but success in those groups didn't grow a person — if he wanted to get better, he would have to make a habit of tackling things that were slightly, or even dramatically, harder than what he was used to.

His parents also taught him how to fail. The by-product of stepping outside one's comfort zone is often failure, and failure breeds experience, and success prior to the failure has a tendency to cause pride. Jake tried hard things and sometimes failed at them, but he learned, improved, or decided he didn't care for it. It was that motivation that propelled him to sign up for hard assignments like Pararescue.

As a sophomore in high school, he was on the verge of quitting basketball until Aiden intervened. The standout senior had come to his aid when Jake needed it most, on the track field defeated by exhaustion. Aiden came alongside and gave Jake the exponential energy of brotherhood. Jake set his will on making the team, that nothing but death could defeat him, and even death would have to take him kicking and screaming.

He had one response when people asked how he was doing: "Good to go." He would say it whether it was true or not. It didn't matter; Jake would make it true or die trying.

Many of the passengers were shaking off the sleeping pills; some looked out the windows. He saw a mixture of excitement and confusion on the new guys. He'd been in their shoes once, but this time was different. Jake had someone waiting for him.

———

The huge aircraft moved up alongside the crowd of mostly civilians with its four engines roaring. It slowed as it passed and came to a stop with its tail end facing the crowd. After several minutes the back ramp lowered and Cynthia strained to see the men clustered above the ramp. They waited for the Air Force crew member to give them the okay, and then the columns of men from one of the Air Force's most elite rescue squadrons moved off the ramp and were home again. Fathers kissed their wives, then knelt down to hug their children. Some of them kissed babies they were meeting for the first time.

Cynthia used her hand to shade her eyes as she looked for Jake among the men. She recognized Kai, and then noticed Jeremy holding a toddler while another boy clung to his leg. She noticed Graciella and Hector holding a kiss that seemed to last forever, girls encircling their legs while Graciella kept one hand on a stroller. Cynthia smiled, and kept looking for Jake.

Right there. He was one of the last off the plane, looking down at his gear. Then he spotted her. She expected him to run up and sweep her off her feet, but instead he walked to her slowly. When he got there he didn't say anything, just hugged her tightly, which was exactly what she wanted.

7

Miles

Aiden pulled into a parking space and sat with the engine and air conditioner running. He looked around him but didn't see Hector's car parked anywhere. He turned off the ignition and a wave of hot air hit him as he got out of the truck to start stretching. There were a few other morning hikers but Aiden didn't expect to see any traffic on the trail, not in this heat. He also didn't expect Hector to accept the invite, although he hoped he would. The squadron had only been home for a few days.

A maroon minivan pulled into the parking lot. Aiden recognized the driver and waved as Hector pulled into a spot a couple of cars away.

"Hey, bro, good to see you again," Aiden said as Hector climbed out. "I thought you might have had your fill of rucking it up through the hot desert."

"Dude, this ain't nothin'. No gear, nobody shootin' at you. Forget it. This is like a sanctuary."

"Where's Graci today?"

"Still asleep probably. But I've been up for hours, time change and all."

"You want to run or hike?"

"I want to see how fast you can get on that thing." Hector pointed to Aiden's running prosthesis. "It looks expensive."

"It probably was but I didn't buy it. It was gift from the

company."

"Good marketing, eh."

"Works great. I had one that didn't before. The tech's coming around. Ready?"

"Yeah, I'll take it easy on you," Hector said, then took off at a brisk run.

Ten minutes later Hector regretted the fast start as he watched Aiden from behind, several paces ahead and holding back but trying not to show it. The trail elevation was gradual, but Aiden was in considerably better shape than Hector, and better on the rocky terrain. The leg device didn't seem to affect him at all. Aiden slowed after what felt like hours to Hector, and they stopped at a lookout point.

Thank God, Hector thought. Aiden was standing, taking a sip of water from the hose of his CamelBak when Hector finally caught up.

"I know you've got more miles on that frame than I do, but geez, man," Aiden said. "I wish I had a picture of you for a caption contest."

Hector was too out of breath to make a witty reply, so he offered up a simple expletive and hunched over to grab his knees while laughing at himself.

"Show off."

"Need a juice box, buddy?" Aiden asked, patting him on the shoulder.

"How about a beer later?"

"You gotta earn it first."

"Alright, alright. How long is this hike?"

"Just ten more miles."

"Screw that. How about we walk back and get a burger. I'll buy."

"Nope, I'll buy. But yeah, we can walk back. Graci would kill me if I broke you on your first week back."

They began the trek down and it was several minutes before either of them spoke. Hector took it all in – the sun's rays, the distant mountains, the peace. It was surreal. Less than a week ago he was immersed in the sights, sounds, and odors of a combat zone. He felt like he could practically see Iraq from where he was standing. Of course, being near Davis-Monthan they heard the occasional jet engine, or saw a fighter once in a while, but it was peaceful. Hector knew he wasn't going to have to run to grab his gear and jump on a Pave Hawk at a moment's notice. He'd get back to training like he always did in a day or so, doing all the same jobs, but with none of the risk of being shot at or seeing barely recognizable body parts in the streets.

He was already set to do some rotations in local hospitals for additional emergency medical training. And even though lives were always on the line there, too, somehow it seemed like a cakewalk compared to his normal routine.

———

Aiden was silent. He knew when Hector had something on his mind; he suspected they might be pondering the same question.

"How's Jake?" he finally asked. He couldn't hold it in anymore.

"You know, he seems fine, but…I don't know. You've known him a lot longer than I have, so maybe you should tell me. You are the expert, after all." Hector smiled.

"Whatever," Aiden said.

"Seriously, you deal with this stuff every day."

"What kind of stuff we talking about?"

"On the surface he's good to go. I mean, you know him. He always does it right. Other guys struggle with hard stuff but Jake's always just got it done, that's the same. But ever since the blue on green with Hondo he's been…vacant, maybe? He doesn't laugh anymore, doesn't joke around. He's just all businesslike. He used to be passionate about stuff. Now he's just…there."

"He lost a bunch of guys that day. Survivor's guilt?"

"We all lose guys. I mean, I'm no doctor, but I don't think Jake has any of that stuff. He was pissed off the way the attack went down like we all were. He seemed to process that like the rest of us. Maybe it's just everything adding up is all. It was a damned mess over there for so long. At least now we've got more to play with."

Aiden knew the pilots killed on Hondo Seven. They were all part of the same rescue group that Aiden and Hector had served in together. The PJs worked with the helicopter and fixed-wing squadrons, such as Hondo, who carried them with the pilots and air crew. Although he was no longer in the unit, they were still his family; maybe even more so, now that he was the one who stayed behind.

They all respected him, loved him even, and though Aiden had more than enough reasons to move on after losing his leg in combat, his place was still here at the base in Arizona, one of the key training and staging locations for the rescue group, caring for the people and their families who were stationed there, including his brother Josiah.

When Aiden heard Hondo Seven was destroyed, he knew Tim and Nathan were dead, and probably their crew chief James with them. He was there to grieve with their spouses and families in the days that followed.

"It was pretty rough here, too. As much crap as we've seen, you just never get used to kids crying," Aiden said. "Tim's daughter is twelve, I think, and she was just a mess. It was hard. I couldn't say anything."

"There's not much you can say," Hector said.

They walked in silence thinking about the last seven years. Hector and Aiden had saved lives together; they'd also killed men side by side. They had watched others die, despite their best efforts to save them. Aiden came home from Afghanistan broken but determined to carry on helping those in need. Hector was wounded, too, but recovered and was later sent to Iraq.

Through all the transitions, surgeries, training, educa-tion, deployments, and honors, Hector and Aiden challenged and kept tabs on each other. Aiden could be totally honest with only a handful of people who knew his flaws and could almost read his thoughts. Abigail and Hector were two of them.

"You should call Jake," Hector finally said.

"I plan on it. I figured he and Cindy probably want to be left alone for a while, though."

"Maybe she'll knock it out of him. That girl is always happy," Hector said.

Aiden remembered the devastation on Cynthia's face at the funerals for the Hondo and Raven casualties. Having married into the squadron a few months earlier she didn't know anybody well, but her heart was broken for them. Aiden noticed her sitting by herself and struck up a conversation in the backyard at one of the family wakes.

He'd met her a couple of times prior to that, always in a group with Jake, in typically rowdy settings. Aiden immediately recognized why people loved her. That day in the backyard as she sympathized with the grieving, she confided to Aiden how unfair it felt for her to fear for Jake, who was still alive, when others had lost everything. Cynthia had never experienced devastation of that kind, but Aiden had, and he helped as best he could, just by listening.

"Nobody is happy all the time," Aiden said.

8

Cynthia

The scream floated like an echo. Cynthia was so tired, the sound seemed a mile away. She half-raised her head when she recognized the voice and started to get up. Jake was already climbing out of bed.

"It's alright. Go back to sleep," he told her. Cynthia's concern faded as Jake walked out of the room. She laid her head on the pillow and was asleep in seconds.

She woke again sometime later to the sound of water running. The room was dark except for the clock on the nightstand with its fuzzy display of red numbers showing 3:45 am. *Why is Jake taking a shower in the middle of the night?* She sat up and rubbed her eyes, then fumbled for her glasses and got out of bed. Light came from the bathroom down the hall. When she got to the doorway she saw Jake leaning against the bathroom counter with the sink running; water was splashed on the floor, and all over the counter. Jake splashed water on his face and head, then paused, staring at the running faucet.

The water was a mess, but Cynthia didn't care. *He's beautiful, and home.* She smiled.

Cynthia took a step toward him and reached out to touch his back. The instant her hand met his skin, Jake exploded.

"Hey!" he bellowed, turning to face whatever touched him with a violent swing of his left arm while reaching with his other hand for any weapon he could find.

Everything blurred. The force from Jake's arm knocked Cynthia backwards so fast she stumbled before her brain could decipher what was happening. The wet floor sent her feet out from under her and she fell, hitting her head on the side of the bathtub and sending her glasses flying. She lay on the floor in shock.

"Oh my God. I'm so sorry," Jake said, dropping the curling iron he was brandishing. He fell to his knees beside her. "Cindy, are you alright? What the heck? I'm so sorry."

She was silent while stars glimmered. They faded and she saw Jake's blurry image. "Yeah, I think so." She sat up and rubbed her forehead. "Do you see my glasses?"

Jake turned off the water, then searched the floor and found them by his feet. He picked them up and they were slightly bent. "Here you go. Dang. Cindy, I didn't mean to, it was just a reflex. I'm sorry. Are you sure you're okay? Do you need me to help you up?" he said, extending his hand to her elbow.

"Yeah, I'm fine. I'm sorry for startling you. I shouldn't have snuck up on you." She sat up. "Why were you taking a shower? Are you feeling okay?"

"Yeah, good to go. I just couldn't sleep, had a headache."

Jake helped Cynthia stand. She was wobbly at first, then looked at Jake, tried to smile. Jake held out her glasses.

Cynthia put them on, "Kinda cattywampus," she said. The frames were crooked on her ears.

"I'm sorry. Want me to try and fix them?" Jake asked

"No, you might break 'em. I'll get them fixed tomorrow. I'm gonna go back to bed."

"You've got a little bump there," Jake said pointing to her forehead. "Want some ice?"

"Yeah, I guess," she said.

———

Jake walked to the kitchen and looked at the previous night's wine glasses on the counter. One was empty, the other still half-full. Cynthia enjoyed wine from time to time, but rarely finished a glass. Jake looked at the red liquid and paused. The female voices screaming in Arabic started up again. He heard them most nights, always waking him up. His nightmares usually involved them in some form or another. Sometimes they were in a helicopter, sometimes clearing a room. He didn't know why these particular voices stuck with him. He'd heard hundreds of Iraqi and Afghan women screaming, often at him, occasionally over dead or dying children. It had never bothered him before — not the way it did now, anyway. He felt sympathy for their loss, but he could detach it as part of the job. He also knew any number of them would kill him in a second if given the chance. He was a PJ because he wanted to save lives, but saving the lives of American soldiers sometimes meant killing others. Jake knew the line between ally and enemy was razor thin, and could change daily.

If it wasn't the screams, it was the man with the mustache. Jake saw him often, staring, smiling. Jake thought about Hondo and the crew he lost as a result of an enemy posing as an ally to lure them in. He could see the eyes of the man he probably would have shot if the explosion hadn't taken out the Pave Hawk, four of his friends, and…how many others? Jake got angry thinking about it.

He pulled an ice pack out of the freezer. He wrapped a kitchen towel around it and noticed a yellow sticky note on the cabinet. *Aiden called,* followed by his number in Cynthia's handwriting. It had been there for two days. Jake had ignored it; he wasn't sure why. Before heading back to the bedroom, Jake took Cynthia's wine glass and emptied it in one swallow.

—

"Here," he said, handing Cynthia the ice pack. She was sitting up in bed with the light on.

"Thanks."

Jake lay down and closed his eyes. He would ignore the headache.

Cynthia took off her glasses and put the ice to her forehead but realized she didn't really need it. She looked at Jake and was filled with compassion. She was sorry she scared him; she didn't know it was possible. He was the strongest, bravest, most confident man she had ever met. He never whined about anything and always exuded confidence. Even when asking her father for permission to marry, he did it without a hint of trepidation. He was charming. He won over her entire family, even her sisters, who took pride in filtering out unworthy suitors.

For six months she'd stared at his side of the bed worrying about him. Her top drawer was filled with notes he'd written to her. Some were printouts of emails he had sent while deployed; some were actual letters still in the original envelope. Most of them were hastily scribbled sticky notes. If Jake had to leave for training while she was asleep — which was most mornings — he left her a note on the bathroom mirror. The bare mirror was much the same as the bare sheets while he was deployed. But now he was back. He was right here where he belonged, and since he was leaving for the base in a few more hours, she would see the sticky notes on the mirror again.

Jake rolled over, trying to get comfortable. She forced a smile, then leaned over and gently put a hand on his shoulder. She knew he was still awake but for some reason he didn't even acknowledge her.

He's going to ignore me? She leaned back, then sat up straight and thought about saying his name, but paused. Jake never complained about being tired. He could stay up all night and get to work on time without any problem. This was new. *What does this mean?*

Last night had been abrupt also. They ate dinner, Jake polished off two glasses of wine, and fell asleep shortly after.

She would have loved to do plenty of things with him, but he didn't seem interested in anything. She would have been satisfied with a long talk, or even a short one, but he didn't even offer that.

She wanted to ask him why he jumped so violently in the bathroom, why she hadn't heard him laugh since he'd been home. Why was he rejecting her now? *Is he just tired? Maybe I should just leave him alone.* He reached over and turned off the light, but for reasons she couldn't explain she didn't move in next to him. She rolled over and faced the other way, but didn't sleep.

Jake's watch alarm went off a couple of hours later. Cynthia kept her eyes closed. She felt Jake get out of bed, heard him getting dressed and walking around the house. Each moment he entered the bedroom she expected to feel his breath to give her a goodbye kiss. Then she would know all was well.

Instead, she heard his keys and the front door closing. He was gone.

She lay looking at the clock for a few minutes, then got up and went to the bathroom. She looked at the mirror. There was no note, nothing but the reflection of a young woman with a red mark on her forehead, tired eyes, and bent glasses.

9

Gridiron

University of Phoenix Stadium

Aiden added his shout to most of the 70,000 people around him. The Arizona Cardinals were up by seven on third and long for the Steelers. The stadium shook with the partially drunken chorus that joined Evan and Caleb McCoy and their uncle. The boys relished the opportunity to yell as loudly as they could, as did Hector's girls. The only person in the row sitting quietly was Stacy.

The Steelers quarterback pulled back and connected for a first down. The crowd silenced and several people threw down their hats. Aiden and the boys sat down in frustration.

"Dang it," Evan said, "We're gonna blow this again like last week."

"Naw, we got this," Aiden said, looking to Hector, holding his youngest daughter.

Hector only grunted.

The Steelers were in the red zone. Roethlisberger snapped the ball, scrambled, and passed to Santonio Holmes in the end zone. Touchdown. The stadium groaned.

"Great," Hector said as he joined in anticipation of impending doom.

"We're still ahead by seven," Aiden said.

"Leinart's a bust. They should stick with Warner. I'm tellin' ya, bro," Hector said.

"We're gonna blow it," Evan repeated.

"What do you think, Stacy?" Aiden asked his niece. She shrugged her shoulders. He was glad she had decided to come, even if Abigail had had to talk her into it. She had seemed happy eating a pretzel and ice cream bar earlier, but aside from those highlights she had been quiet. She didn't bother standing and didn't yell. Stacy rarely yelled. She was happier on the way there, sitting in Hector's van with his daughter, who was probably the only reason Stacy had agreed to come.

"I'm gonna run to the bathroom," Hector said to his girls. "Here, help a guy out, bro," he said to Aiden while handing over the baby.

"Whoa there," Aiden said.

"Come on, man up. You can take on the Taliban and five patients, but you can't handle a one-year-old? She eats and poops, you'll be fine. I'm bursting," Hector said as he moved down the line of people.

Aiden laughed. He was familiar with babies.

———

Hector turned into the tunnel leading to the concessions and headed toward the bathroom. Throngs of people had the same idea, trying to relieve themselves of the beer and soda before the Cardinals' next possession. Earlier in the game they had already run back a kickoff for a touchdown, so the odds were against missing another one. Hector hurried.

He got to the bathroom and found the stalls occupied, so he went to the trough urinal, moved to the far corner, and waited until a spot against the wall emerged. Hector felt someone behind him and was instantly uneasy. *Too many people. I'm boxed in.* For a moment he hardly cared about the game, he just wanted out of there, and fast.

Hector made a cursory pass under the faucet with his hands, didn't bother drying them, and was in the open again, but not enough. He kept going until he reached an abandoned ketchup and mustard stand, and turned his back to the wall.

He knew there were no threats around him but he couldn't escape the instinct. There were no IEDs in the garbage cans; nobody was going to jump out of the beer garden with an AK-47. But he could not shake the alert status learned during years of combat – large crowds needed to be dispersed, because large crowds hide bad guys. Bad guys blend into crowds. Blind corners hide bad guys. Hector was a veteran, a pro. *Maintain situational awareness* was one of the first lessons learned, a lesson he taught to the men below him.

Hector was always on alert but he could mask it from his family. They never noticed him give hard looks at sketchy guys. He didn't fear them; he kept a concealed pistol at all times, just in case. But guns we're not allowed in football stadiums, so Hector had to leave it in the car. Now he felt unprepared.

The minute he stood there felt like an hour. Eventually the smell of the pickle relish and the roar of the crowd snapped him back, and Hector remembered the greater threat: Aiden holding his baby girl. He got back to his section and saw Aiden on his feet rocking the baby.

"You alright there?" Aiden asked.

"Yeah. I fell in," Hector said as he wiped his hands on Aiden's back. "Three and out, huh?"

"Yup," Aiden said, handing the baby over.

"Kurt Warner, man. I'm tellin' you. We've got the pieces," Hector was glad to be thinking of something else.

Much to the delight and relief of Evan, the Cardinals managed to hold off the Steelers' comeback for the win. The seats emptied as the spectators moved to the inevitable traffic jam getting out of the stadium. Aiden and Hector let the kids run around the empty seats while waiting for the traffic to die down.

"Jake blew you off, then?" Hector asked

"I never talked to him. I left a message with Cindy and sent him an email about the game, but he never wrote back."

"I mentioned it to him. He just said 'okay' and went on to something else," said Hector.

"I'll go over to his house tomorrow."

"Yeah, see if you can get anywhere, 'cause some of the other guys are noticing, too. He's even getting snippy with Kai. I don't want some Chair Force Lt. Colonel writing anything up. I need him back in gear. We'll be back over there before you know it."

"Right," Aiden agreed. "But you know as well as I do what Jake is gonna say."

"Good to go," they said at the same time.

Cynthia was reading on the sofa when the doorbell rang. When she opened the door, she was surprised to see Aiden behind it.

"Hey. I was hoping to catch Jake but I don't see his truck…I'm guessing he's not here?"

"No, I haven't heard from him." She immediately kicked herself for saying it. She didn't want to badmouth Jake.

Aiden gave a surprised look that Cynthia noticed.

"Do you know when I might catch him?"

"I'm not sure what his schedule is these days. I guess it's kind of sporadic."

"He didn't tell you when he'd be home?"

"Not always. Your schedules are all over the place, right?" she asked.

Aiden wanted to tell her no, that she should expect to know where Jake was, but decided to keep it to himself. He didn't want her to worry, nor did he want to cause a rift between them. But it was frustrating.

"Well, he never got back with me and I was hoping we could catch up." Aiden paused. "How is he? How are you?"

Cynthia wasn't ready for such a direct question. None of her friends were military wives. All of them were excited that Jake was back, and they stopped calling her after he returned. The ones she ran into at work smiled and went on about how great it must be to have him back safe. Cynthia put on a fake smile and agreed. She was upbeat by nature, and she honestly didn't know who to take her concerns to.

Jake had hit her, but it didn't happen the way others would see it. Her sister would certainly not understand. Her brother-in-law worked in an office, didn't know military types. Cynthia had only known Jake for less than a year when they got married. Her parents loved him, but maybe they might start questioning her decision to marry him so soon. She didn't want to open that can of worms.

She made the mistake of looking into Aiden's eyes, and she lost it. Tears started flowing and she had to turn away. Aiden wanted to comfort her but knew better. The same caution that kept his feet planted on the porch rather than accept her invitation inside restrained his desire to help. Cynthia needed someone to talk to, but not him.

"Cynthia, you don't know me well, but I've known Jake a long time. If there's something going on with him, I want to help if I can. And if there's something going on with you, whether related to Jake or not, I also want you to be able to speak to someone who gets it."

Cynthia looked at Aiden. "Thank you. It just seems like he's not…happy. I don't know if it's depression or if he's just changed, but he used to laugh and get excited about stuff and now he's just…he's just not himself."

"I think some of the guys in his unit are noticing it too. So just know, we've got his back, and yours. Okay?" Aiden pulled out a pen and pad and scribbled a number. "This is my sister-in-law's number. Her name is Abigail. My brother is a pilot and she's dealt with this stuff for years. If you need someone to talk to, give her a call. Alright?"

Cynthia wiped her eyes. "Okay. Thanks."

Aiden wanted to say something else but was at a loss for words, so he smiled and nodded before turning away. He drove his truck to the end of the street before pulling over and taking out his phone.

Abigail's voice picked up after three rings. "Hello?"

"Hey, sis, you may be getting a call soon."

Cynthia stared at the computer screen without interest; she was thinking. She had already written in her journal, read some books, and read her Bible before she finally called Jake, and he didn't answer. After that she called her sister, but she couldn't bring herself to broach the topic. Naomi had problems of her own, so Cynthia mostly listened and encouraged her, and deflected most of her questions.

The note Aiden left was still next to her keyboard. She picked it up for the fifth time and looked at Abigail's number, but in the end she decided to use it as a bookmark.

Four hours after Aiden knocked on the door, Jake pulled into the small driveway. He walked in and saw Cynthia sitting on the sofa with her book and a mug of tea.

"Hey, I'm so glad you're home." She got up and hugged him. "I was worried."

"Sorry. Don't worry about me," he said, matter of fact.

"I'll worry if I want to, but I probably wouldn't if you'd called. Where were you?" she asked, trying not to sound angry.

"Work. Why? I'm not out cheating on you, if that's what you're thinking."

What? She tried to shrug off the odd comment. "I know you have a crazy schedule, but you have a phone, right?"

"Sorry, I'll call next time," Jake said, and went to the bedroom.

What the hell? He's never walked out on me before. Now she was angry. She followed him, getting more heated with every step.

"Not even going to kiss me? 'Hey, Cynthia, how was your day, I love you so much'…nothing?" Her voice was rising as she spoke, and her tone was getting sharper.

"Why are you yelling?"

"I'm not yelling."

"Sounds like it. I already said sorry."

Oh, don't even. She thought about pulling back and letting it go. She'd been taught to walk away when you're angry, but she didn't want to. *I've been conciliatory for weeks. When is he going to do his part?* This was not the man she'd married. *Would Dad ever treat Mom like just another roommate? No, never. Would mom put up with dad being a careless jerk? No.* Gary McMillan had taught his daughter to ride and shoot at the age of seven, and she wasn't accustomed to disrespect.

"If you want to hear me yell, I'll do it. Believe me, you don't want to." They made eye contact and stared at each other, neither sure how the other would react, or what to say next.

"What do you want from me?" Jake finally said.

She wanted him to pick her up and kiss her. She wanted him to let her know she mattered. She desperately wanted Jake to love her, to court her like he used to. She wanted him to smile, just once even. She didn't know what to say, so she sat on the bed and silently prayed.

Jake knew he should walk over and sit next to her. He wanted to but something stopped him. Instead he just stood looking at her, and then turned away. She might be crying but she was being discreet. He saw a box of tissues on the nightstand and knew he should grab one, go over to her, and hug her. He knew he should apologize and ask her forgiveness. He knew there were a thousand things she needed, but instead he just stood there.

He was not a quitter, and for a moment he realized that standing still was quitting on Cynthia. He decided to go to her.

Why is he just standing there? He's just going to watch and let me cry. This is not Jake. I want my husband back. Cynthia remembered Aiden's words, his compassion for his high school friend. *Maybe Jake needs to talk with someone other than me. We can't do this forever. I can't do this anymore.* She finally decided to say it.

"Aiden came by today."

Jake stopped in his tracks. "What are you talking about? What do you mean, he came by?" Jake was almost scared to hear the answer.

"You never called him back, so he came to see you."

"So, what, you and he just hung out, had some nachos?" His tone was insulting.

"Give me a break, Jacob. He didn't even come inside. He's been trying to reach you because he cares about you. Maybe if you called back your friends –" Cynthia got up and moved toward him, and her eyes burned up the tears that never came. "I don't know what it is. Ever since you came back you just seem…" She wanted to say *rude*, or *depressed,* or *a jerk* but decided to finish with "…absent."

"Absent," Jake repeated. He was losing his patience. He imagined Aiden standing in his front yard, listening intently to his wife, probably giving her that sympathetic ear he was known for. Everybody loved Aiden. He was quiet, but he was always there for his friends, and even strangers. Jake loved him, but not today.

Perfect. Aiden was here doing what he does best, taking care of others. Taking care of my wife. He lost it.

"Hey, if you want to call Aiden, be my guest. Go out, see a movie, run off to Vegas and have at him. I'll be here when you get back. Because I don't quit on you. You want to go, there's the door. I ain't going anywhere."

Cynthia couldn't hold back the tears anymore. This was not going at all like she'd planned. "Jake, that is ridiculous. I can't believe you'd even suggest that there's something…I've only had, like, two conversations with him." She paced to the nightstand and stood in the corner. *This isn't Jake. What do I do?*

"What do you want?"

Cynthia said nothing. She was done.

"I'm asking you. What do you want? Tell me."

No response.

"Well, then I'm going to go take a shower and eat something. If you come up with an answer, you let me know." As he left the room, he blurted out, "Or call Aiden, if you'd rather."

Cynthia sat for a long time. Long after the shower had been running, she finally opened her eyes and stood up. She walked back to the living room and found the book she had been reading when he got home. Cynthia closed her eyes and took a deep breath, then pulled out the bookmark and reached for her phone.

—

"I love that girl," Abigail said.

"Yeah?"

"She's nice, like really nice. Like if I were super-nice and sweet, she would make me wonder if I was doing something wrong."

"You're nice…sometimes."

"Watch it."

Aiden smiled, but leaned away. "Am I wrong?"

"I'll take off that other leg if you don't behave yourself, and use it to knock some sense into that friend of yours."

"What'd she say?"

"He's a jerk."

Aiden raised an eyebrow at her.

"I get the guy's been through a lot, but he should be thanking his lucky stars he landed that girl. And she's no pushover either. I mean, you know some women will doubt themselves, and try to make excuses for him. Not her. She knows she's not doing anything wrong. He's just being a jerk."

"You know there's more to it than that."

"Maybe he's messed up, maybe he has full-blown PTSD; I don't know, you're the expert. But I also know sometimes a guy just needs to man up and treat his wife like she's more than just a fixture. He's got problems, he's having a hard time adjusting or whatever, fine. Do something about it and stop treating your sweet wife like a doormat. I mean, she said you called him and went over there and all. Has he taken any steps? Shown any responsibility?"

"Not with me."

"Exactly. What happens, happens, but some of what happens *after* that…that's on him."

"I can't force him to sit down and open up. From what I hear, he's still crushing it from an operational standpoint. He's on a short list for some sweet assignments. If he's doing the job, he's doing the job."

"Well, maybe Hector should force something. Isn't there a protocol for this stuff?"

"A lot of guys are reluctant, commanders too. For one, it means you're acting like a pantywaist."

Abigail looked at Aiden. Her eyes disapproved.

"Not me, but it's the reality. A lot of the guys think that way, especially the more elite units like the ones knocking on Jake's door. We're taught to be aggressive and set all that namby-pamby stuff aside. It's trained out of you, so nobody wants to be *that guy,* who can't handle it when it goes down. Hell, you know. Josiah was always cocky, even after all he went through. And from the command side, it totally depends on the commander. Some officers don't want to hear it. They say suck it up or get out."

Aiden took a sip of water. Abigail looked away.

"I had one guy tell me that after seeing me, his guys came back acting like pansies. Some will intentionally brush stuff under the rug, or reassign guys they don't trust or don't want to deal with. Bury them in a desk somewhere. Others will do whatever it takes to get their guys back on track. When my team went over there last year, the base commander considered us essential personnel, so you just never know. Doesn't matter how high up you go, a guy never knows what to expect by going to his commander and being honest."

"So what's Hector doing about it?" she asked.

Aiden didn't answer. He didn't know.

10

Triage

The car radio displayed 3:50pm. He was going to be late for work, again. He'd been out too late the night before. Again. The traffic was light during the afternoon so he might be able to make up a few minutes if he hurried. He pressed on the gas.

The approaching intersection showed a green light that would turn yellow any second. It did. He switched lanes to get around the cars braking in front of him, gunned it, and flew through the intersection.

Whew, made it. Just a few more miles. I might make it on time, after all.

He smiled and relaxed, but soon found his way blocked by the rear of a large tractor trailer. He slammed his fist into the steering wheel and cursed, then switched to the right lane, neglecting to check his mirrors and almost clipping the car in his blind spot. The other driver laid on his horn but he paid no attention.

He saw another yellow light, the cause of the semi's deceleration. It would turn red any second. He didn't have time to stop for a light; he accelerated his Mazda past 90mph.

The light turned red long before he was even close.

A Suburban approached the intersection to his right. The woman driving saw her light turn green and moved her foot back to the accelerator as she started her right-hand turn at the intersection, and never saw the little blue car coming from the left where it shouldn't have been, and merely saw a blue streak on her left before it disappeared in a cascade of glass.

The Mazda's front right fender glanced the SUV's front left. Glass and steel flew in every direction. The Suburban spun to the right, made a half-rotation and settled to a stop across the turn lane.

The light Mazda hit the heavy SUV with enough kinetic energy to redirect it at a 45-degree angle from the collision. It hit a concrete barrier which sent it airborne and spinning into the opposite side of the intersection. It collided with a pickup truck as it landed, knocking the pickup on its side. The Mazda spun upside down until it smashed into the embankment, four lanes away from the Suburban.

Inside the SUV, the young mother was stunned by the violence of the impact. She sat in the dust cloud, staring at the airbag when wailing cries reached her and slapped her sensible. She unlatched her seatbelt and climbed over the seat, little cubes of glass cutting into her hands and through the knees of her jeans, adrenaline hiding the long-term back and neck injuries she wouldn't feel till later. She got to the center seats to check her children, snug but terrified. The back of the vehicle was relatively unscathed, but she scrambled for the latches on the car seats in terror nonetheless.

Then she smelled it. Something was burning.

Within the inverted Mazda a young man hung unconscious. The seat belt seemed determined to pass judgment on its driver, holding him in a firm grip within the disfigured anemone of sharp steel and glass, while smoldering remnants of months of discarded fast food packages combined with the fumes from the now-broken bottle of vodka, intended for tonight's after work festivities. The fire grew exponentially, consuming the back half of the car, on its way toward the employee who would never be late for work again.

—

"You comin' tonight?" Kai asked.

"I don't know, maybe," Jake said.

"Maybe, meaning 'Shut up and don't ask me about it?'"

"Sure, that works." Jake smiled, then added, "Cindy's not into bars."

"So, she's into food right?"

"Wings and fried onions don't fire her up like they do you."

"Don't lie. I ain't seen you two anywhere lately."

"So?"

The question hung in the air as Kai pulled his truck to a red light. Jake sipped his soda in the passenger seat. He knew it was true. He also knew he was lying about Cynthia. She wanted to know his friends and their wives better. They'd be deploying again in six months, maybe four. Cynthia felt she was part of a family she hardly knew, and the funerals after the Hondo attack hammered it home. If something happened again, she wanted to share in the loss and assist in the healing. It could very well be her own husband next time.

Jake and Cynthia hadn't gone out with the guys since the group's return. Sports bars didn't appeal to either of them, but Jake usually kept tight with his teammates and Cynthia enjoyed most of them. Leslie and Kai invited them over to their place twice, but both times Jake told her no, forcing Cynthia to turn down the offers. It annoyed her; she didn't want to offend Leslie. Jake knew she was right and the argument afterward reinforced to him that he was blowing it with his wife. But he just didn't want to be around people. He couldn't explain why, nor did he want to.

Jake watched the traffic through the windshield and saw

a blue car streaking toward the intersection diagonal to them.

"Whoa, Kai. See that?"

They watched the Mazda enter the intersection, smash into the Suburban, and spin toward them. It slid up a concrete barrier and flipped over, flying toward the pickup in front of them and knocking it over as sparks flew across the hot pavement. Jake reached into the back of the extended cab, pushed their workout bags out of the way, and grabbed Kai's med kit.

"Check them," Jake said, pointing to the Suburban. "I've got these." Kai vaulted over the concrete barricade and approached the front of the Suburban.

Jake saw the truck's driver had unbuckled and was trying to open his car door from the inside. "You alright, sir?" he asked, holding the door open so the man could climb out. He didn't appear to have any injuries other than some small cuts.

"I think so," the driver answered.

"Hang tight and sit over there. I'm gonna check on the other driver," Jake said.

As Jake rounded the truck, the familiar smell of burning trash and vehicles engulfed him. The smoldering debris in the back of the Mazda caught and in seconds the hatchback was in flames. Jake saw the mangled body of its driver upside down, still buckled. He couldn't tell if he was alive or dead. He called out, "Can you hear me?"

There was no response. Jake tried the passenger door handle. It moved but the door was too mangled to open. Jake wished for a crash ax, a tool he could have used to cut a hole in the side of a helicopter, standard gear in Pararescue. He got in between the driver side door and the wall and tried to pry open the door. Two additional men came up behind him to help. Their combined strength opened the door, but the heat from the fire was increasing. Jake got on his belly and slithered over the glass through the open door as far as he could reach and felt for the seatbelt buckle as he also felt the heat and worried he might be burning, but he kept at it. He strained till he felt the end of the belt, then the button, and pressed it. But the tension was too great; the button wouldn't release.

Jake slid backward and hollered, "Hey, I need a knife! Get me a knife."

One of the men pulled a knife off of his belt, opened it and got down to reach into the side door to give it directly into Jake's hand. Jake took it and sliced the seatbelt as the smoke stung his eyes. The driver fell free and crumpled onto the ground as Jake tried to support his head and neck, and he got a hold of his armpits.

"I got him, pull us outta here!"

The other men pulled Jake's legs from behind, though the smoke forced them to do it with their eyes closed. Jake heard sirens approaching as they pulled him out of the side of the car, but there were only a few feet of clearance before the concrete divider, the men struggled to pull Jake and his patient across the pavement, toward the back of the car. Once they were thirty feet behind the flaming vehicle they let go, coughing violently, as Jake rolled onto his knees and shook the glass and debris from his bleeding legs and torn clothing before kneeling next to the driver.

He was bleeding from the nose and mouth, and his face had multiple lacerations, peppered with glass and rock fragments from the road.

Pulling his body from the vehicle probably exacerbated spinal injury. Don't worry about it now. Assess the damage.

———

Across the intersection, Kai looked into the window of the Suburban. "Anybody hurt in here?"

The children were crying but their mother yelled over them. "I think we're okay. Can you help me get them out?"

"Yes, but you're bleeding, ma'am," Kai said as he opened the passenger door and looked over the terrified toddler. "You're alright, buddy, it's alright. Here, sit tight while I check on your brother." He turned to the mom. "I'm EMT-trained, ma'am. Just sit tight while I check them out. Try not to move too much, alright?"

"Okay," she said. "It's gonna be okay, baby, we're alright," she said to her boys.

Kai gave a quick check on the other boy, trying to ignore the smoke building around them. He looked him over, unbuckled him, and pulled him out of the vehicle.

Setting him on his feet, he said, "Buddy, this smoke is bad. Don't breathe it, okay?" The boy nodded and followed him around the back toward his mom. The first ambulance began weaving through traffic to reach the accident. The fire trucks were farther out, negotiating the roads.

———

He's bleeding from the ears. Skull fracture? Probably spinal damage. Doesn't matter, he's not breathing. Jake kept the man's head in a neutral position and moved around to kneel at the top of the man's head. Jake got on his elbows, put his hands on the sides of the driver's head to grasp his jaw from both sides and move it forward. The man's tongue moved out of the way, but his chest was still. Air was not flowing. Jake had to get air into his patient, and fast. He looked around for his pack.

"Hey," Jake hollered to the nearest person he saw. "Bring me that pack. Right now, quick."

The driver of the tipped-over truck was holding a rag to his neck, but he picked up the pack and hurried to Jake, kneeling next to him. He unzipped it and held it open for Jake while staring at the bleeding man in front of him.

Jake reached his hand into the pack and rummaged around until he caught hold of pocket ventilation mask. He lifted the man's jaw into the plastic mask and let it seal over his mouth and nose. As Jake squeezed the bag he could see air was entering, but there was almost no exhalation movement and it sounded labored. Something was wrong. *Probably crushed his lung, or lungs, in the crash. The trachea is shifted to the side.* Jake felt his pulse. *Heart rate is low. Pneumothorax?* He folded back the man's shirt and saw the discoloration on his chest. There was air trapped in his lung; he needed to ventilate it. Jake reached into the bag for a chest dart, and heard the ambulance somewhere behind him. He looked up at the guy holding the bag.

"Wave over that ambulance. Bring them here."

The man dropped the bag and stumbled to his feet, thankful to get away from the blood and the smoke. Jake pulled out the syringe/catheter contraption and found a good spot to insert. Two paramedics came up and knelt next to Jake, conducting their own assessment. They could see he was trained. One of the firefighter/EMTs knelt next to him.

"I'm Ethan. What do you have?" he asked, eying the vehicle more than the patient.

"He's breathing but his left lung needs to be ventilated. Pulled him out of that car so we need a board," Jake said, inserting the syringe. The other EMT assisted Jake while Ethan stabilized the patient's neck and administered breaths with the bag.

"What about the other vehicle?" Ethan asked surveying the scene, trying to take in the circumstances of the accident, thinking through the mechanism of injury.

"My buddy is on it. I don't know."

"Go check on them," Ethan said to his partner. "We'll get him ready to move."

The dart worked to release the air and the patient began breathing. Jake started to treat the bleeding; he figured there was head trauma from the blood pouring out his nose, so he held the bandages firmly, though not applying pressure for fear of causing greater damage.

Ethan looked at the inferno that used to be a blue Mazda. The firefighter in him was worried. They were directly behind the burning vehicle, in exactly the wrong spot.

"We need to move him. Get the backboard from our ambulance. I've got him," Ethan told Jake.

———

The other EMT approached Kai, who was holding a bandage against the woman's temple. "How we doing?" he asked.

"Minor lacerations on Mom from cut glass. Kids are fine."

"Alright, I'll check them out," he said. Kai was grateful to hand them off. He was worried about Jake.

Multiple sirens and fire truck horns shooed cars out of the way. The first ambulance was parked off the road next to Kai's truck, and Kai saw two fire engines in the distance as he walked toward Jake through the smoke.

Jake stood up. He had cuts and scrapes of his own now, and there was blood on his clothes but he didn't notice any of it. Ethan was still kneeling next to the driver on the ground.

"Need to get a backboard out of their rig," Jake told Kai.

They went to the back of the ambulance, opened the door, and had just retrieved the backboard when they heard an explosion. Instinct and training drove them both to their knees, and they reached down for harnessed rifles that weren't there to confront the source of what they'd heard.

Gunshot?

IED?

What the hell was that?

———

When the 2004 Mazda spun to a stop upside down, its rear hatch fell partially open and the friction of the steel on the intersection's pavement threw sparks on the greasy trash inside the car, as well as the oil residue from the driver's never-washed apron and hat, and ignited. It may have burned if not for the broken bottle of vodka. While the fire crew was still maneuvering their engine to the scene, the fire grew hotter every second, and soon it burned at over 300 degrees. By the time the PJs got to the ambulance's rear door, it was above 500 degrees.

The Mazda's rear hatch was supported by two elongated struts, facilitating the mechanics of opening and closing the hatch. When they got hot, the gas inside them expanded and built immense and increasing pressure until they reached 284 degrees, at which point the tubes could no longer contain the pressurized gas nor the small metal rods attached to them.

Roughly thirty feet away, Ethan knelt next to the patient, working the breathing device, when the Mazda's strut blew, sending a rod of chrome hurling through the air with the force of a rifle shot.

Ethan was a seven-year veteran of the fire department, and secondary explosions from a fire were not a mystery to him. He heard the explosion and knew what it was before he felt it. The hot metal rod flew straight through him, ripping through his bunker pants and every successive layer it encountered: clothing, skin, the edge of his femoral artery, and back out the front of his pants where it ricocheted off the ground and finally sank three inches deep into the concrete embankment off the side of the road near Kai's truck.

He felt the pressure in his pelvis and knew he was in trouble. He also knew he was probably in shock because he didn't feel any pain yet. He felt for the wound and was shocked by wetness in his pants.

Ethan started to get lightheaded and fell onto his left elbow. With his right hand he instinctively put pressure on the front of his thigh. He passed out after six seconds.

———

Jake and Kai knelt side by side, scanning for threats. They felt exposed, on the defensive; it was never a good place to be. Their training led them to move and take the initiative, and they got back on their feet. Jake was first to spot the EMT on the ground, lying face up and bleeding. He saw the other patient's breath bag wasn't moving on its own. *What's going on?*

A second explosion erupted, and a streak of blue smoke whizzed between the PJs like a bottle rocket.

"What the hell was that?" Jake said.

"No clue. Fireworks?" said Kai.

Great, we're gonna die by assault from the world's smallest RPGs. They wondered how many more of the beastly little things were going to fly out of the burning car.

They reached Ethan and the volume and color of the blood told Jake it was an artery. He felt in the hole of his pants, then tore it open with his fingers. Kai grabbed the scissors to widen it and the PJs pulled the bunker pants apart. The location of the hole confirmed it. He pulled on a pair of gloves from Ethan's pocket and searched for other holes while Kai took over ventilation for the downed driver with one hand and leaned down to listen to his breathing.

Jake tried to apply pressure to the artery. *Tourniquet? No, the wound is too high. Maybe a high tourniquet, pressure on the femoral to control it? Think, Jake. Work the problem.*

Jake stuck his left finger into the wound, pushed against the artery while searching his med kit with his right hand, and pulled out a wad of combat gauze. He took his finger out of the wound, wrapped the end of the length of gauze around his finger and shoved it back in until he felt the artery. Jake unrolled another six inches of the length, fed it to his finger, and shoved down the hole on top of the other gauze. Like a human sewing machine he packed most of the roll into the wound six inches at a time, a fluid motion that was as natural to him as breathing.

The EMT's partner, alerted by the explosions, came up to Jake as he was flaying back the edges of Ethan's wound so the folds of skin would help keep the gauze in place when released. The pseudo-gunshot wound was packed and both patients — one of which was now strapped to the backboard with the other EMT's assistance — were ready to move in less than a minute.

"Here, slide him over," someone said to Jake.

Jake realized they were surrounded by the legs of firefighters, and he felt the spray of water as it doused the flaming vehicle behind him. Three firefighters hoisted the driver, and four more took their colleague before Jake had even stood up. He repressed his possessive tendency over his patient; he understood the firefighter's zeal to take over from two guys in Under Armour workout clothes.

Jake and Kai receded from the drama playing out around them as actors taking their exit from the stage. Both patients were lifted into separate ambulances. There was debris everywhere, running diesel engines, flashing lights, and rough men going about their business. There were also on-lookers as far as the eye could see, and so many firefighters and police that the PJs felt in the way.

Kai retrieved his pack. A couple of cops noticed, and took them aside to get statements before they left.

Kai looked at Jake and shook his head. "Good to be home, huh?"

Jake couldn't tell if he meant Iraq or Arizona; everything was eerily similar to the last six months.

"Right," Jake said. As they walked toward Kai's truck he noticed something protruding from the concrete barrier. Moving closer, he saw the strut stuck in the concrete and reflected on the irony of living through multiple deployments at war only to almost get killed by a random piece of metal a few miles from his house.

They climbed back into Kai's truck, now stuck in front of a line of cars backed up from the closed intersection. They realized they might be stuck for a while and cranked up the air conditioning to wait it out.

Jake took a sip from his soda — still cold, still full of ice. It dawned on him how fast everything happened, and was over. *Ten minutes? Maybe five?* Jake remembered Kai's invitation. *Maybe getting out, being around people laughing and having fun wouldn't be so bad. I could unwind after this.*

"Maybe we will come tonight."

Jake walked into an empty house that evening. "Cindy?"

He was in a good mood, his first in weeks. The day's events invigorated him, reminded him of a good kind of routine, good because nobody died. He felt…proud. Jake lived to save lives, something he did routinely in far flung locations, but never at home. He never experienced the satisfaction of being able to do what he loved and then come home and share that satisfaction with his wife. He envied those firefighters. He wasn't one to brag, but part of him wanted to tell Cindy about it. She would be proud of him. He tried to tell himself it didn't matter, but everyone wants to hear, "Job well done" or have their wife brag about him. Jake had never heard Cindy brag about him, though she did it all the time.

He changed clothes and went to the kitchen, where he saw a sticky note on the counter:

Never got a call from you. Went to Naomi's for dinner. Be home later. I love you. – C

Jake kicked himself for not calling her to tell her he'd be late, again. *You had a good reason this time. Now she's going to be pissed. Great job, Jake. This is not how tonight was supposed to go. Nothing is the way it should be anymore.* Every day brought some new level of suck. Even today with things to celebrate, he was the bad guy. On deployment he had saved hundreds of lives. *Is this what they come home to?*

Jake knew he should pick up the phone, call Naomi's house. He should go over and apologize and tell them about his day. *No, they won't get it.* They would ask all sorts of questions he didn't want to answer. He'd have to tell a tale, and he didn't do that. He didn't tell war stories. He wanted to relax, have fun, drink a beer, and forget about the day, not relive it with wide-eyed outsiders who would ask a bunch of dumb questions and smile, calling him a hero. *Screw that.* If he went to Naomi's, he'd be miserable. Maybe not on a normal night, but tonight…

No thanks.

Jake put the phone down. Instead he took a shower, changed, and grabbed his keys. Jake looked at the note on the counter and knew he should write one of his own, stick it to the bathroom mirror. Instead, he scribbled a detached post-script into the margin of Cynthia's: "*Me too.*"

I think I've earned some slack.

And he walked out again.

11

Thursday

Aiden pulled into the busy parking lot. The place was hopping, and he had to circle around to the side of the building to find an open space. It wasn't his type of environment, and he felt foolish for being there. The rowdy bar scene never appealed to him much; Hector didn't care for it, either. But they had been invited by Matt, and neither of them got to see him much. Aiden had been Matt and Hector's sergeant once upon a time, and now they each had more tours than Aiden. Most of the guys at the bar tonight were only casual acquaintances to Aiden, but they all knew him, or at least, they knew his…legend.

As new faces emerged from the Pararescue training pipeline and his friends dispersed, he began to feel more and more like an outsider. Most were getting married, having children; Aiden had neither. He was Uncle Aiden to his brother's kids, played plenty of Legos, but he wasn't a dad, wasn't a husband. He didn't seem to fit in anywhere. He traveled a lot and was often distracted from a foreboding loneliness with speaking events and conferences of every kind.

Which I should be preparing for tonight. He was flying out Friday afternoon for a speech on the East Coast, but Aiden still hadn't connected with Jake yet, even to just say hi. Aiden hoped Jake would be here tonight; it was really the only reason he'd come.

The noise hit him when he walked through the door,

and he searched for familiar faces. He walked around trying not to notice the glances of patrons, themselves trying not to stare at his leg. He felt on display and was about to leave when he was slapped on the back.

"How you doin', Sarge?" said Matt.

"Hey! Good. I've been standing around like an idiot, though, looking for y'all." Aiden said.

"We're over there," Matt said, pointing to a block of three tables in a corner. "And I gotta find a bathroom."

He stumbled away and Aiden headed toward the group. Among all the guys were four ladies, including Graciella, and Kai's wife, Leslie. Aiden knew all but one of the men, and was glad to see Jake.

"Aiden, thank God," Graciella said. "Now we can stop listening to these kids ramble on about video games," she said while giving him a side hug.

"Or the freakin' Red Sox," Hector said.

"There's the door, old man," one of them replied, pointing.

"Oooh, look at that TV, so exciting. Find a real sport."

"Just because you can't even hit a softball..." Everyone laughed, including Graciella.

"I didn't want to play on your stupid softball team, but you turned her against me," he said.

"No, we only wanted Graci. We just asked you to be nice," Jake said.

"It's true," Graciella noted.

Aiden sat next to her, across from Jake. "Hey, Hector got a few hits that season. He almost had a heart attack running to first, but he got a few hits." The table laughed at Hector's expense. Aiden gave a head nod and a smile to Jake, who acknowledged, but released eye contact right away. A cry of exclamation rocked the bar area as spectators reacted to the baseball game.

"Who's watching your girls?" Aiden asked Hector.

"Doubled up with Matt's," he said.

"Who's doubling up with Matt? I ain't doubling up with anybody," Matt said with a moderate slur.

"He means the babysitter," Kai said.

"Oh yeah, they're with my ma," Matt said. "She ain't used to that many kids, though. They probably have her tied up by now."

"No, your girls are so sweet," Leslie said.

Hector and Graciella scoffed in unison.

"Yeah, sometimes, but lately, Papa comes home and they get all crazy. I almost left them home with Hector and came myself, but Matt's mom said she'd watch them all. God bless that woman." Graciella turned to Hector. "Which reminds me, you said you'd take me dancing tonight."

"So, I hear you're heading out of town in a couple days," Matt said to Aiden.

"Yeah, I'll be in Florida on Saturday."

"What for?" Kai asked.

"Giving a speech for Wounded Warrior Project," Aiden said.

"Are you a veteran?" one of the ladies asked. Several of the PJs smiled.

"What, you've never heard of the great Aiden McCoy?" Jake said before Aiden could answer. His tone was mocking, but it wasn't directed at the woman who asked. Jake was staring at Aiden. The jab took the air out of the room. Jake didn't know why he said it. Part of him wanted to take it back, but another part of him wanted to let loose in a manner two less beers could have restrained. The young lady was embarrassed and looked at her friends for help.

"Google his name. You'll be impressed," said Jake.

Another jab. Everyone looked at Aiden, wondering how he would respond. Would he laugh it off or get offended? They knew Aiden and Jake were old friends, but they also knew Jake was acting out of character, and had been for weeks.

Aiden McCoy was not quick to anger. He was the last

person on earth to start a fight, and only Hector knew he could finish one. Every man at the table had absolute respect for Aiden; several had served either alongside or under him, and those who hadn't loved him for other reasons.

This time Aiden was angry, though he didn't show it. He had compassion for Jake but his patience was worn thin. To be ignored by a long-time friend in whom he had invested so much time was frustrating, but he understood the reasons. But to be publicly ridiculed by that friend was something else entirely.

Aiden almost stood to walk out, but quitting wasn't his character any more than it was in Jake's. Aiden lived his life by the Pararescue motto *That Others May Live;* it guided his decision to join the Air Force, infused him with resolve on the battlefields of Afghanistan, and directed him into a career in counseling so guys like Jake could function even after enduring war and everything it brought along with it. Aiden would never quit on his men, and he wasn't going to quit on Jake. Whatever pain Jake wanted to spew onto others, Aiden was willing to take – but mastering his passion was an art he was still learning.

He took a breath, and summoned the maturity that age and sobriety provided. He turned his attention to the young woman. "Yes, I used to be in Pararescue, along with most of these guys. But that was a while ago." He smiled at her.

Everyone sat a little more comfortably, except Matt, who stared at Jake. Matt and Hector had a bond with Aiden that few men did. And like Aiden, they were older and more mature, but Matt lacked sobriety.

"Kinda pissy tonight, eh, Jake? What, Cindy kick you out for being a jerk?"

"You still here, Matt? Isn't this about the time the bouncers kick you out so you can stumble home…to that empty house of yours?" said Jake.

"Lay off, Jake," said Hector.

"Maybe if Matt'd laid off a little more, he wouldn't have

crashed and burned with Heather." Jake and Matt locked eyes.

Kai was Jake's best friend, but even he was done. Guys teased each other mercilessly, but wives and children were off limits and Jake knew it.

"Jake." Kai said it with an authority that stopped the conversation in its tracks. "Shut up."

Jake took a sip of his beer and looked away. Both guys backed down, for now. There was a long silence at the table. Aiden hoped someone else would chime in, but it was clear everyone was tense and unsure of what to say. He decided to try engaging Jake.

"So Jake, I heard your sister is tearing up the court this year."

Jake blinked and looked at Aiden. "What?"

"Kierra, right? She and my youngest sister are on the same basketball team. They're both seniors. They got pretty tight after the accident." Aiden said.

"What accident?" Jake asked.

"They got into a pretty bad car accident a few months ago. Nobody told you?"

"First I'm hearing about it," Jake said. *Thanks a lot, Cindy.*

"Sorry, I figured your parents told you." He paused. "They were both fine, but had to go to the E.R. for lacerations. Been friends ever since. I was back home last summer and spoke with a bunch of them. I think they were both looking into enlisting, but I don't know how serious they were."

"I'm gonna find a bathroom," Jake said, getting up.

Aiden watched him walk away. He looked at his untouched glass of beer.

Matt looked at Kai. "Why's your buddy such an ass lately?"

"How about you shut up too, Matt, alright?" said Kai.

Leslie rubbed Kai's shoulders, Matt took another drink, and Hector and Aiden looked at each other.

———

In the bathroom, Jake splashed water on his face, then did it again. He stared at his reflection in the mirror. *Was she just trying to make things easier by not telling me? That must be it.* Cynthia was always upbeat in her emails and phone calls. She never complained about anything, always told him things to lift him up. Jake appreciated it, but another part of him was pissed.

She's treating you like a kid; doesn't think you can handle yourself. She thinks you're weak, it said. Jake knew it wasn't true, but the accusing voice continued. *They all think you're weak. You've been a jerk, too. Aiden knows it. That's why he's here. You're just another messed up vet he wants to fix.*

Jake wrestled with the voice. Aiden always had gone out of his way for Jake. When Jake was the little sophomore in the crowd full of seniors, Aiden had made sure to include him. Jake chose Pararescue over college basketball because of Aiden, who mentored him throughout his training and answered every email, even during the early days of the war in Afghanistan when communication stateside was sketchy at best. When Jake was struggling to pass the PJs' medical exam that crammed two years of college study into mere weeks, Aiden took precious time to coach Jake through.

When Aiden lost his leg, Jake was crushed. When Aiden won his medals, Jake was proud. So many people chastised Jake and Cynthia for eloping, but Aiden had sent them the most generous and thoughtful gift they'd received.

No, Aiden is a friend. He's always been a friend. And you're being a jerk to him. You're being a jerk to everybody. You tell people you're good to go. You're a liar. What's wrong with you?

The bathroom door swung open and a man walked in. Jake shrugged off the train of thought and finished drying his hands and face.

———

Graciella tugged on Hector's sleeve, "Okay, this has been fun. Now it's time to have my kind of fun." She smiled.

"Lead the way, baby. Want to go to a nice dinner, no kids to keep from climbing under tables?" Hector looked at his watch: 19:30. They still had three hours of babysitter left.

"No, let's just grab some drive-thru and then go dancing," she said.

"I guess we're outta here, bro," Hector said to Aiden. "Sorry to leave you with the kids."

"I think maybe I'll head out, too." Aiden looked around. "It was nice to meet you guys. Have a good night."

"Yeah, you too," several voices said.

Leslie, sitting in Kai's lap, watched the three walk away and spoke what was on her mind. "It's not just Aiden, he's pissing all over Cynthia, too."

"He wouldn't hurt her," said Kai.

"Not physically, but she's always sad now, and he's always a prick."

"He was awesome today. Give the guy a break. Unless any of you pulled a guy out of a burning car and saved two people's lives like it was nothing, then I say, button it."

Leslie stood up. "Oh, I know you ain't talking to me right now."

"Come on Les, the guy needs a break."

"I think I need a break, too. Excuse me," Leslie said as she walked away.

Kai lowered his head and swore into his glass. Matt and the others laughed.

Thanks a lot, Jake, Kai thought.

———

"You should stay. Maybe he's got it off his chest now?" Hector said as they walked toward the door.

"No, Matt's pretty wasted. I don't wanna poke the bear.

Besides, I gotta pack anyway."

"Sorry about Jake, but keep at him. I don't know what else to do. Hopefully he'll come around."

"Maybe I'll catch him on the way out. If you talk to him, let him know he can come by anytime," said Aiden.

"Will do. Peace, bro."

Graciella gave Aiden a hug. "Have a safe trip."

"Thanks," Aiden said. He decided he'd hit the bathroom before he left and maybe see Jake for a second, say goodbye. *Maybe if there isn't an audience…*

Aiden saw Jake before he got there. "Hey, I was just gonna take off, but I wanted to let you know, feel free to call me or come by anytime. Even if you just want to hang out or play some ball or whatever."

You're just a project for him. Maybe Aiden will even use you as case study in his speeches.

Jake didn't answer. Aiden spoke into the awkward pause.

"I'll be out of town till late Saturday night, but seriously, call or text me anytime. I care about you and Cynthia." Another pause. "Well…good night."

Aiden walked away.

Jake almost broke through the accusatory wall. He wanted to apologize to Aiden, to everybody, but the second Aiden said Cynthia's name the voices returned and he imagined Aiden holding Cynthia's hand, comforting her through the hardship he'd brought upon the lively woman. Jake was a monster, and Aiden was the knight.

He watched Aiden walk out the doors. Fury overtook him and he followed Aiden with his eyes through the windows toward the back parking lot. Jake stood transfixed for what felt like an eternity, and then he rushed out the door.

———

Hector and Graciella closed the doors of their minivan.

Graciella wished the van had a bucket-style front seat like Hector's truck instead of captain's chairs; she wanted to move up close and snuggle her man as they drove. She was so relieved to have him back for a while.

He could have taken a medical discharge when he was wounded in Afghanistan, but he had fought through the pain of physical therapy in record time. She helped him with simple, intimate tasks during his recovery and was frustrated when he went right back to it — first when he returned to Afghanistan, then to Iraq, where things seemed to get worse every year. And Hector, she knew, was always in the thick of it. He told her everything, because she wanted to know.

They were from a rough neighborhood, and growing up, Hector was always in on the action. He was also first to throw down. Hector never backed down from a fight, and Graciella was angry at times but also impressed because he had always fiercely protected his family, even against guys twice his size. Hector wasn't afraid of much; not her Dad, brothers, or cousins. He wasn't afraid of threats from gangbangers, nor was he afraid of fatherhood. In all his life, Hector had only ever admitted fearing two things: Graciella and her grandma.

Graciella looked at her husband across the three-foot span of the minivan's front seats. She wanted him. For so many months she had wanted him, here, doing exactly this. The hours of wanting and praying were finally over.

Hector pulled into a fast food parking lot and drove around to the side window. "What do you want, baby?"

"Whatever you're getting, I don't care." And she truly didn't. All she wanted was to hold him, dance with him, and love him.

"Alright, let me see." Hector leaned out the window to speak into the intercom when he noticed movement behind his car. *Something's not right.* He paused and looked back. There was a man walking with dark clothing across the drive-thru lane. Hector leaned back in, looked into his rear-view mirror, then turned and tried to make out the figure. It was standing still, holding something. *A cell phone?*. Hector's heartrate skyrocketed. He began to sweat.

Graciella noticed he was spooked. "What's wrong?" she asked and looked over her shoulder. She saw the figure. "What, a homeless guy?"

Hector's hands gripped the steering wheel. He turned it slightly to the right, away from the building. A small car and its three teenage occupants came to a screeching halt behind them. The headlights made him wince and it lit up the mini-van interior. *Get out of here now.*

He pulled the wheel hard to the right and gunned the gas, and the minivan jumped out of the lane and over a curb. Graciella shrieked. The van bounced over rock and bush landscaping adjacent to the drive-thru lane, and once clear, Hector accelerated even more and weaved through the parking lot and onto the street.

Graciella yelled in Spanish. Hector kept weaving through traffic and accelerating.

"*Hector!*"

He heard his name and snapped back. He looked around and realized he was going 70mph, and let off the gas.

"I'm sorry. That car just came up on me so fast. I…I'm sorry."

"Baby, it's okay, but you scared me. What were you afraid of?"

He didn't know what to say. He wanted to explain to Graciella how everything scared him, how a piece of trash on the side of the road was a roadside bomb, how a sudden vehicle rushing where it shouldn't be meant an attack, how every man holding a cell phone was waiting to detonate an IED, that crowds were dangerous, and anything happening suddenly meant it was time to act, to fight, or to get the hell away. *How can I tell her that? How can I ever explain that to her?*

"Talk to me, Goose," she said, and half-smiled. "I've never seen you scared, baby, but it's okay. Tell me."

Hector blinked away a tear. *Tell her.*

"Look Graci, I know you want to go dancing, and I want to take you, but would you mind if we just got a cup of coffee first?"

"Of course." Graciella reached over and caressed his hand on the wheel.

For the next three hours they sat at a booth in a quiet diner. He spoke, she listened and asked questions and held his hand the entire time. Hector told her stories and her heart broke, but she was happy, and strangely, so was he. It was all that either of them wanted to do.

———

Aiden looked at his watch and was partially relieved to be leaving early. He'd only gone to see Jake, but that had failed miserably, and Aiden hated failure as much as he hated lies. It was lies, he was convinced, that created all the problems. It was a series of lies that threw him into confusion. The lies he heard while sitting in his hospital bed looking at the bandaged stump of what had once been his leg told him he was a broken, inadequate failure. Aiden rejected it, every day, for years. The lies tried another approach, telling him he no longer had anything to offer the men he cared most about. They were over there, deployed, and he couldn't help them.

But that lie overplayed its hand. Aiden heard it so much that he made the mistake of voicing it over lunch one day to the toughest man he'd ever met in his life, a SEAL lieutenant, who set down his fork, folded his hands to keep from pounding the table, and looked at Aiden for a full minute before speaking.

"Aiden," Porter had said, "that's about the biggest load of" [expletive, expletive] "lies I've ever heard a badass" [expletive] "like you spout out in my entire career. Don't ever say that" [expletive, more expletives] "to me or anyone ever again."

Porter unfolded his hands and leaned back in his chair. "You need a mission to matter? Okay, I get that. There are plenty of missions all around you. Get on it, because the guy who lost that leg doesn't [expletive] walk away from the wounded. You still him?"

Porter didn't create the will in Aiden, he just stoked the ember that was always there.

Aiden focused all his energy on learning new methods of healing and walking alongside those in need, helping them overcome the lies they believed about themselves, along with the physical and mental challenges. It was the reason he pursued Jake and others, even strangers. He knew what it was like to despair, to feel lonely, and Aiden got good at spotting them in a crowd. Aiden too was often lonely. For all of his family and friends, accolades and awards — and there were many — even in his celebrity, Aiden was lonely. But he never stopped caring, and never let his circumstances get the better of him.

Maybe Jake needs to hear it from someone else? Give him space.

As he stepped along the dark sidewalk he wrestled with conflicting emotions of pity and anger. Aiden knew Jake better than anyone. At least, he used to.

"Hey." He was surprised to hear Jake's voice behind him. "Cindy's at her sister's house, in case you're looking for her."

Aiden was dumbstruck. "Ah, no. I wasn't. Why would I be?" Aiden was offended, and didn't hide it. He was running out of patience.

"Good, so stay out of my business and stay away from my wife. Got it?"

Aiden summoned one last measure of restraint for his old friend. "Jake, I don't appreciate what you're insinuating. I respect you, and your wife. I wish you both the best. I'm going home." Aiden turned and walked away.

"Oh, of course, the perfect Aiden McCoy is above reproach. Jake's the hothead. Aiden is everyone's best friend. He's also the best friend of everyone's wives, too."

Aiden knew to stay silent. He knew Jake was saying things he didn't believe – at least, he hoped so. He would disengage and let him cool off. But then Jake started up again.

"Of course, he can't get a wife of his own, so he stays home, the shoulder to cry on, while their men are getting all dirty in the big sandbox." Jake hated saying the words, but he couldn't control it.

Aiden turned on his heel. He stared into Jake's eyes and took three rapid steps toward him. The men were face to face and Aiden's eyes flared. Jake could feel Aiden's breath. He had never been afraid of Aiden before, but he was now.

Aiden wanted to grab Jake's throat, or punch him in the jaw. He fought the mockery and took a deep breath. His anger was toppling over, stifling his self-control, but he managed to get out a single word.

"Goodnight." He turned away, his heart beating faster than it had in years.

How dare he turn his back on me again? All of Jake's frustrations poured out on the only available outlet, and he grabbed Aiden's shoulder and pulled him around.

"Don't you turn your back on me!"

Nobody had touched Aiden with aggression in years and his trained response was action. Before he could think about what he was doing, he threw Jake's arm off and caught the edge of his chin in the process. The act was so swift Jake reacted in kind, bringing his left arm around and punching Aiden in the side of the head. Aiden absorbed the blow, but instinct and training told him to protect himself by countering the attack. He threw a punch of his own.

Jake grabbed him and drove him into a car door. The commotion attracted onlookers who dialed the police. Aiden tried to push Jake off him and in the process whipped into another car, grappling. Jake threw another punch that dazed him, and he stumbled to his knee.

Two bouncers came from around the corner. Jake saw them, and looked at Aiden kneeling in front of him, a hand on the car's hood for support. He thought about what various commanders had told him over the years. *I don't care how rowdy you get on your free time,* they said, *but don't break the law, and don't put me in a position of having to deal with your crap.*

Jake knew staying put might mean getting arrested. Getting arrested might mean…he didn't know. Fear had been in charge all night and fear told him to run. Jake obeyed the lie again, and ran.

Aiden was still on the ground when the police cars pulled up, sirens squawking. They never saw Jake.

The officer looked Aiden up and down, noticed his prosthetic, and wondered who would get in a fight with a guy with one leg.

"Are you in need of medical assistance, sir?"

Aiden got to his feet but didn't answer, looked away.

"Can you tell me what's going on tonight?"

Aiden knew he should be polite and comply but he was too emotional to be coherent. He didn't want to talk; he didn't want to answer questions.

"We have witnesses who say you punched the other guy in the face and you both started fighting, smashing into cars."

Aiden looked away.

"Who's the other guy?"

Aiden didn't say anything.

The officer shrugged his shoulders, figured the guy would eventually cooperate, but for now, the situation contained too many unanswered questions. There was damage to vehicles, and witnesses, and probably another side or two to the story.

"We'll sir, put your hands behind your back. I'm placing you under arrest."

Jake didn't stop till he was three blocks away, and then ducked into a busy shopping center. He slowed his pace and walked the aisles till he was in the back corner of the store, where he fell to his knees and cried.

12

Friday

"Mr. McCoy?"

Aiden opened his eyes but hadn't been sleeping.

"Yes, sir?" he said.

"Come with me, son." An officer held open the cell door, and Aiden walked out.

"To the right." The man motioned down the hallway and followed Aiden, directing him into a small office area. A second police officer was doing paperwork and a third poured a cup of coffee.

"Have a seat, Mr. McCoy," the first officer said.

Aiden sat at a desk across from him. The other officers paid no attention to them. The station was quiet except for some music playing on a computer nearby. The officer looked over the papers on the desk.

"You've never been arrested before, is that correct?"

"Yes, sir."

He put the papers down and leaned back in his chair, clasped his hands behind his head in a casual manner and looked Aiden over before speaking.

"Want some coffee?"

It was the last thing Aiden expected to hear. He wanted coffee, but wasn't sure why he was being offered it. "No, thank you, sir. But thanks for the offer."

Aiden felt awkward under his gaze but didn't know the protocol. The officer had a curious expression as if he were unsure what to make of the young man sitting across from him. "Why are you here, Mr. McCoy?"

"Beg your pardon, sir?"

"I asked why you are here, son."

"I was arrested for getting into a fight. I don't recall the specific charge."

"What I mean, Mr. McCoy, is that you kinda get a handle on who deserves to be in here and who doesn't." He paused, waiting for Aiden to reply.

"Yes…Sir?"

The officer continued, "I seen a lot of guys in stupid bar fights. Some of your guys, too. Believe me, Mr. McCoy, you don't fit the bill."

Aiden sat back. He didn't feel like talking about Jake or about the fight, but the officer was using a tone Aiden recognized. It was the tone Aiden used when speaking with a new client, a personality willing to listen, seeking to help. It was disarming. "Sir, I made a mistake, lost my composure, and I regret it. I apologize for my actions. I assume the judge will let me know the consequences."

"Ain't gonna be no judge, son."

"I don't understand."

"Ain't nobody pressing charges, except maybe the guy whose car he says you scratched. The piece of junk was already all scratched to hell, though."

"I don't want any special treatment."

The officer laughed. "Mr. McCoy, I don't mean to offend you, but in the grand scheme of Tucson's criminal justice system, you and your friend's little scuffle doesn't exactly register. I've got a unit bringing in a guy who almost beat someone to death; they had to chase him down. I got three junkies tweaking in cells down the hall. If you'd been willing to talk to the officers at the bar they probably wouldn't have even arrested you. And believe me, nobody wants to deal with the publicity that comes with charging a Medal of Honor winner. That's just a fact. Technically, you're free to leave. I was just curious if there might be more to the story."

Aiden felt stupid and ashamed. "I'm sorry. Sorry for causing you all a headache." He stared at the wall, and the officer stared at Aiden.

"I had to look up your name because it seemed familiar. I remembered I once saw a speech you did at a Fourth of July VFW event."

Aiden remembered the speech, and the boy scouts and veterans he'd met that day. "You're a veteran?"

The officer nodded. "Nam and Desert Storm. Army."

There was another silence. Again, the older man broke it, "So, now that we've had our little bonding moment, what are you doing here, Mr. McCoy?"

"I just lost my temper."

"Why did you lose your temper with a friend? Girl?"

"Negative, sir. What makes you think he was my friend?"

"Because JSOC guys like you don't end up with baby scratches when they go at it for real. Somebody gets bloody, and they break a hell of a lot more than some yuppy's feelings over his scratched-up Subaru."

"Yeah, I suppose that's true. You've been a police officer for a while then, I take it?"

"A loooong time. What's going on with your buddy?"

Aiden wanted to tell him, wanted the wisdom of another point of view from a man who'd lived it, but Aiden didn't know what the outcome would be for Jake.

"I'm afraid I can't say, sir."

"Oh, I know you don't want to reveal his name and all, afraid he might get bumped down a rank, or whatever they do these days."

"I don't even know." Aiden paused before going on. "I do counseling for veterans, see a lot of guys who have a hard time transitioning. It's pretty surreal flying out of a battle zone in the morning, and being back home tucking in your little girl that night. Some people, no problem, others…it's just too much. He's like that, I guess."

"So he just pissed you off?"

"It was a misunderstanding. It happened so fast, it was just…a mess. Now it's probably worse."

"Ya think?"

"I wanted to help him, instead I clocked him."

"Maybe he deserved it?"

"It doesn't exactly help with his therapy."

"And you?"

"What do you mean?"

"Who's going to help you out? You're not married. Girlfriend?"

"No, sir."

"Why not?"

"I just haven't met her yet, I guess."

"Well, you ain't gonna meet her in here." The officer stood up and motioned to the door. "Down the hall, all the way to the end. They'll buzz you out, give you your wallet and stuff."

"Thank you, Officer…?"

"Stram."

"I appreciate it, Officer Stram. I won't be back, I assure you."

"Keep doin' what you're doin', son, except for the fist therapy and all. Next time you want to punch somebody, find a gym."

"Yes, sir."

———

Aiden walked out of the police station. It was morning, but just morning enough for the streetlights to shut off. He held his keys, wallet, and phone in his right hand and fumbled to get them sorted. He wondered where his truck was until he realized it was still parked at the bar. He looked at the phone. Its battery was on life support, but he might have enough left to call…*Hector, no, not Hector, maybe…no, not Abby. A cab.*

As he looked up the number in his phone, he noticed someone walking toward him. It was Abigail. For several strides she moved fast, but something stopped her before she got close enough to speak, almost as if she were afraid to complete the distance. Aiden couldn't discern the look on her face; it was one he hadn't seen before. She nodded for him to follow her, turned, and began walking back to her vehicle.

Aiden trotted to catch up. "Abby, I'm sorry to drag you out here. Thanks for coming."

Abigail McCoy whipped around. She looked Aiden in the eye for three terrible seconds, and then slapped him across the face.

Aiden was stunned. His world was in flames and he dared not speak. He didn't need to; Abigail wasn't done yet.

"What the hell am I doing standing in the parking lot of a police station at the crack of dawn, Aiden? Why the hell am I getting a phone call from Cynthia saying Jake never came home and she's worried he blew his brains out?"

With each question her voice got louder, angrier. "And I can't call *you* because your phone just rings, and now I'm all freaking out and call Hector, who says you were with Jake last he saw you. So then I get on my knees and start praying, and what happens next, Aiden? After like an hour of back and forth with Cynthia, Hector calls and says you got arrested in a bar fight. Seriously, Aiden?!" She rubbed her forehead with her hand and paced near a light post, reloading.

"And then I have to get Kaitlyn to come over and stay with the kids. Oh, and I can't tell her why, of course, and then bring my frumpy hair out here to intercept you, because Hector doesn't get to cover for you, Aiden. I swear, I almost called Grandpa because I know he would have laid into you, but not enough. You're all mine."

At this she almost smiled, and then continued. "And I have to figure out a way to tell my boys that their uncle, who they admire almost as much as their Dad, is sitting in some urine-stenched cell because he punched one of his friends in the face."

How did Abigail know it was Jake?"

Abigail read the question in his eyes. "Oh, of course Hector won't say who it was because you all have this code or something, but we can read the tea leaves. Don't forget, I've been dealing with your type since I was a kid. What do you want me to tell Evan? Stacy? Sorry, sweetie, Aiden just has no self-control anymore. Why?" She was almost shouting.

Aiden had no words. Abigail continued. "They know you're not perfect, believe me. So do I, but you have a freaking responsibility and it extends beyond you! You have three kids at my house who are terrified of their Dad getting blown out of the sky halfway across the world because, you know what? It happened once before. Remember?" she said, gesturing to Aiden's leg.

"They need you to be better than you. They need you to be safe, and they're not the only ones. How many kids have you lectured to since you got that blue ribbon placed around your neck? For better or worse you have to bear it. And I'm going to be sure you do, because I love you and your damn brother, and I'm sick of having to do this crap on my own!" Abigail threw her coffee on the ground, splattering her latte across three parking spaces. She ran both hands through her hair, and wiped tears from her eyes.

Aiden stood transfixed. He had only felt this ashamed and inept once in his life.

Abigail put her hands on the top of her car, pressing her forehead against the driver's side door. After a brief prayer she stood up straight, opened the door. She felt the way one does after throwing up after hours wrestling with nausea. It wasn't a good feeling, but it was over and a relief. She had needed to get it out. Now she could breathe.

"Come on." Her voice was softer, and tired. Aiden obeyed.

They buckled up in silence. As Abigail pulled out of the parking lot she reached toward the cup holder before remembering her latte was currently feeding bugs in the police department parking lot. Aiden noticed and thought about speaking but didn't. He and Abigail were stuck in silence. Neither of them knew what to say. Abigail decided to put her foot down one more time.

"I'm going to get another coffee before taking you back to your truck…and you're buying." There was a hint of humor in her voice again.

The tension lifted, slightly. "Yes, ma'am."

Abigail's frustration from a lifetime of stress and worry had finally boiled over, but she forgave Aiden, and Josiah, and she wanted him to know it, but wasn't ready to tell him yet. Not until she had another latte.

Maybe I should feel bad about slapping him? Then she remembered the daddy long legs' he dumped down her sweatshirt as a kid. She smiled.

Nope, it felt great.

Aiden set the cup of coffee on the counter and plugged in his phone. When the battery showed a charge, he saw notifications for dozens of messages and missed calls. He turned it off and pushed it away. Opened the refrigerator, realized he wasn't hungry. He lay down on the sofa and closed his eyes; he'd been up all night but he wasn't tired. Aiden wanted to break something, or unload a magazine…or run.

He downed what was left of the coffee and filled his CamelBak, then shoved a chocolate muffin in his mouth, forcing it down. He started to pick up his phone but paused, and decided to leave it. He had to catch a plane in the afternoon and didn't want to talk to anybody.

He stepped out the front door. A few stars remained in the sky. He hit the pavement and was warmed up by the time he reached the intersection. Aiden rarely ran in the city and wanted desperately to get away from people. He increased speed and headed toward the hills.

There were a few parachutes in the distance to the north, men practicing jumps in the frigid dawn, preparing to do things he used to do — should be doing — things he longed for. Aiden ran faster.

The music in his ear buds wasn't loud enough to drown out regret so he turned it up, all the way up. Three songs later he reached the outskirts of town. His aggression controlled his pace and the elevation only made him go faster; he set his will on conquering it. A thousand thoughts flowed in, and then flowed out just as quickly. He didn't want to deal with any of it, was tired of dealing with it. He was tired of being positive, tired of processing other people's problems, tired of being the strong one.

He didn't want to get on the plane to give another speech — not to school kids, or businessmen, soldiers, or senators…anyone. He wanted to jump off a helicopter. He wanted to dodge a hail of bullets and pick some bleeding soldier off the battlefield. He wanted to matter. He wanted in on the action.

Aiden wanted to be over there with his brothers, all of them. They would get shot and he wouldn't be there to help. Aiden wanted to scream. He ran faster.

He came upon a trail head with a closed barricade, pummeled over it barely breaking stride. The chords of U2's Ultraviolet played in his ears. Aiden stumbled and fell, landed hard on the sandy trail and felt the scrapes of a bloody elbow. He smashed his fist onto the ground and got up more pissed than he'd ever been in his life, scrambled up, and ran even faster. He wasn't thinking, or dreaming, or even regretting now; he had simply succumbed to fury and was laying on the gas.

All the years of training for Pararescue, all the missions, injuries, deaths and saves — they flooded by him in a blur. The surgeries and awards, accolades and nightmares all flew past him. He was almost at the end of the trail, and wanted to launch right off the edge of the cliff at full speed, but instead he slowed. The city was magnificent in the first rays of morning. The desert colors of cloud and sunrise mixed into a beautiful tapestry that only God could design, and Aiden inched closer and closer to the edge.

Aiden thought about his friend. *Screw Jake,* he decided. Aiden thought about Abby's slap. *Screw Abby, too,* the voice said.

But no, it was another lie. Abby was right. His heart agreed, and ached. Anger, resentment, regret, none were the proper response; it was grief. Aiden decided to let himself grieve for his friend, for himself, for his brothers, for everyone. He looked east and grieved for Josiah's little girl, and for Josiah, who was desperate to see her. He grieved for the marriages destroyed, for the men he dealt with every day, for the families of the suicides he'd encountered. Aiden grieved for the Afghan civilians he saw slaughtered by the Taliban, and the innocent caught in the violence of war, for firemen and airline passengers in burning jet fuel and crumbling skyscrapers, and for the complacency of those who didn't seem to care anymore; and Aiden grieved for Abby and for Cynthia.

Aiden fell to his knees and let out a wail over the treetops, over the city. The tears streamed from his face and hit the dirt as he wept, and the sun shone on his shoulders.

———

Cynthia heard the key in the front door and leaped up from the sofa, and was there before it opened. Jake paused when he saw her but couldn't look her in the eye.

"Baby, what happened? Where have you been?" She was crying through the words. There was not a hint of anger in her voice.

Jake tried to speak but he had no voice. What could he say? What would she understand? How could she understand? Even Jake didn't understand. A voice told him to blow her off

— to shrug past her and tell her to leave him alone. *What's wrong with me?* She was asking the question he wanted answered as well. *What happened? And why?* He didn't know what to do. He was lost.

Suddenly Cynthia was tired of waiting. She was tired of waiting for Jake to come around. She saw someone she loved in peril; she was determined to save him. She thrust herself against him and hugged him with all her strength. She cried, and held, and prayed…and waited.

Tell her, a different voice told him.

But she won't understand.

That's right, she won't…yet.

"Where were you all night?" she asked.

"Nowhere. Truly, just nowhere, sitting in my truck for hours, thinking about how to fix things."

Cynthia waited for him to continue.

"I punched Aiden." Jake expected her to recoil but she didn't. She held firm. "He didn't do anything wrong, I just lost it and he happened to be there. Then I ran…like a coward, I ran away. I couldn't come home and pretend. I couldn't make sense out of it. I still can't. I'm sorry. This isn't what you signed up for."

Cynthia absorbed it, then spoke, still holding him. "It is and isn't. But I'm here, and we can figure it out together, so long as you're willing to talk. Nobody can help us if you won't. Don't give up."

Jake didn't have a clue where to begin, but he had no options. There was nothing to hide behind, no way to blow past it. He had to trust Cynthia. He decided to lay it on her. Cynthia listened as he described as best he could the anxiety, the inability to relax like he used to. He described the Iraqi man with the mustache he saw almost every night in his nightmares. He told her about the screaming in the dark, and the images of war he never imagined he'd see, like a mere child so bent on killing Jake that he was willing to use his little brother as a shield. Jake lived in a world of savagery and didn't know how to convey it.

But Cynthia understood human nature, maybe a little better than Jake. He was familiar with the face of evil but not its origins, nor its antithesis. Cynthia understood both. She wasn't shocked by anything he told her. She was appalled and saddened, not at him, or anything he did, but by the reality of a fallen world and the fact that her husband would be going back into the hell of it. Despite her own self-interest she wanted him to, because he was great at it and they needed him.

In that instant, she recognized her role in the war they were fighting. She couldn't help him with what he did over there, but she could encourage and strengthen him here, and help him fight through things she was willing to learn about. She wanted to be part of it, to contribute to him becoming better at everything he did.

Jake and Cynthia spoke in quiet voices all morning. Eventually they were able to laugh, and eat, and truly enjoy being together again for the first time since before his deployment. They acknowledged it wouldn't be easy, but Jake and Cynthia Lyons were not the type to back down from a challenge.

Later that evening Jake stood in front of the phone. He'd been avoiding the call all day but knew he had to make it. He dialed Aiden's number.

The phone rang several times before Aiden's voicemail picked up. "The caller you are trying to reach has a mailbox that is full..." Jake hung up. Even if he could have left a message, he wouldn't. He knew he had to speak with Aiden. He was finished making decisions out of fear. He was not going to back down from this, either.

13

Saturday

Aiden took the stage to a mostly standing ovation. Only those in wheelchairs, and there were several, remained seated.

"Ladies and gentlemen, thank you for inviting me here today. I know many of you in this room are no strangers to a fight. Many, maybe most of you, have been dealing with combat for most of your adult lives. First it was on the field of battle, only to come home to a fight of a different kind. I've been there, you've been there. I'm not here to tell you my story, you can read about that elsewhere. I'm here to help all of us engage in that secondary battle."

Aiden walked around to the side of the podium, making eye contact with a number of people in the crowd.

"This is a different kind of fight, one that takes place in the mind, but one that destroys lives every bit as often as an IED or a stray AK round.

"When I returned home, I was fortunate enough to travel around the country and meet a lot of you, veterans from this war and others. I also got to meet people in various stages of trauma, not just military but across all walks of life — from a parent who saw his son killed by random violence in Nebraska, to a woman dying from a disease the doctors had no answer for, to commanders who've lost whole squads to a single well-placed explosive.

"I met a beautiful nineteen-year-old girl who lost both legs and much of the right side of her body trying to figure out how to feel important again." He paused to let the image simmer, then dropped his voice. "Nothing will be easy for her — for any of them, or us, ever again," he said, surveying the audience.

"All I ever wanted to do growing up was help people. Don't get me wrong, my brother and I loved blowing stuff up," he paused for the laughter, "but he does it much better than I do. Whenever people got a little injured, I got a little giddy. I loved patching them up. It's why I joined the PJs, and it's why I went back to school and endured the drudgery of a lecture hall. I love reading, but I want to be where the action is. What I learned from my travels is that there are wounds that aren't obvious. Not to diminish the loss of life or limb, but trauma also takes another toll. It takes our ability to feel safe, and ultimately for others to feel safe around us.

"You are all aware of the Walter Reed scandal. It's been in the news all over the place, and I get as angry as you when I think about veterans and their families getting left behind. We should never leave a man behind. Not over there, and not over here." Aiden paused for the applause to die down.

"I no longer have the ability to bring them back from over there. There are plenty of men and women, some of them good friends of mine and yours, who will do that. But we can play a part and ensure they don't get left behind here, on our own soil.

"How many of you have heard of the Army's Mental Health Advisory Team? There were some startling findings I'd like to share with you, and also some things we've been doing lately I'd like to talk about."

Tucson, AZ

Aiden was exhausted. The past 48 hours had been a whirlwind. He'd been too worked up to sleep on the Friday afternoon flight to Florida. Important people whose names he wished he could remember had picked him up at the airport and taken him to dinner. By the time he got to his swanky hotel, it was after 11:00pm. Then he'd been up early on Saturday for breakfast and a tour with VA hospital staff, followed by several other low-key meetings.

He was always glad to connect with people in need, but their stories drained him and his tank was already on fumes. During the entire trip, he vacillated between being angry at Jake and worried about him. Aiden also worried about Abigail, and everyone else important in his life. It was almost easier to be out of town, but he also felt like a coward who'd run away from his problems.

By the time he had finished his speech Saturday afternoon — and shaken the last hand, exchanged the last phone number, and taken the last picture — there had been barely enough time to pack and catch his late flight home. He declined the offer to stay in Florida through Sunday to enjoy a football game. The commander and team officials had invited him to take part in the pre-game festivities, and Aiden was used to that kind of thing, but it would have meant more pictures and handshakes, and he just wanted to be home.

He ignored all of his emails and voicemails. He needed to deal with them, but he was spent. He planned to crash into his bed, do nothing on Sunday, and recharge for whatever Monday might bring.

He pulled into his driveway, turned off his engine, and sat. *Maybe I'll just sleep here.* He enjoyed the silence for a minute, then climbed out of his truck and walked toward his porch. He was so tired he hardly noticed the dark figure sitting on his front steps waiting for him. When he did, he stopped in his tracks.

"Do you remember the first thing you ever said to me?"

He recognized Jake's voice.

"No, not really. I remember it was in the locker room."

"I was sitting there thinking about taking a shower and feeling sorry for myself. I'd had the worst practice of my life. You walked by me and patted me on the shoulder and said, 'You're getting beat because you're backing down. Push back.' And then you walked away. That was it. You never spoke to me again till that day on the track. I wanted to be you."

Aiden kept his distance. "Why?"

"You know why," Jake said as he looked up at him. After a second he looked at the ground again. "Everybody loves you. Even the people who hated you respected you."

"It was the same with you," Aiden said.

"People tolerated me because I forced them to. I made sure they knew they needed me, but they wanted you around. Everybody has always wanted a piece of you. I know, because I did too."

Aiden knew it was true. He'd been dealing with it non-stop for the past thirty hours. He wondered what Jake was doing here, at this hour. He didn't seem like a threat anymore.

"Jake, I'm sorry about the other night. I lost my cool, and…it was just completely out of line. Please forgive me."

"Holy crap, Aiden, there you go again! See, that's it. That's why, because you're always the good guy, everybody's best friend. It's so selfless, it's nauseating. You couldn't even let me be the one to apologize first. Do you get how annoying that is?"

"Jake, I don't know what to say." Aiden dropped his backpack into the dirt and laid down right there on the ground next to it. "I don't know what to do, and I don't…What do you want?"

Jake was surprised. Aiden was never distraught.

"I wanna go inside and use the bathroom, for one thing." He gestured toward the six-pack next to him; two bottles were missing their tops. "I got tired of waiting foryou."

Aiden smiled. He reached over and pulled a bottle out of the carrier, got up, and unlocked his front door.

Five minutes later Aiden was lying on his sofa, staring at the ceiling when he heard the toilet flush. Jake came out and sat on the opposite sofa.

"Better?" Aiden asked.

"Much."

"Is there anybody you need to call? Let 'em know where you are?"

"Cynthia knows I'm here. In fact, she's the one who insisted I come." He paused. "Why she puts up with my junk is beyond me. When I got home yesterday, I lost it. I was so tired of it all. I blabbered it all over her."

Aiden listened, his silence inviting Jake to continue.

"She just kept hugging me. It was surreal. I've been the worst husband, a crap friend. I trampled on her for weeks, and what does she do? Hugs me and holds my hand and kisses me. I don't even know how long I talked, hours maybe. She just stayed there and absorbed it all, and we…it was good."

Aiden smiled. "Jake, you're one of the most talented men I've ever known. Everybody knows it — Cynthia knows it, Hector knows it, the Air Force knows it. We all know you're going to get bumped right up the chain any day now, and we want to see you there, varsity level. Those guys need your skill."

Jake peeled the label off the bottle, looking down. "It's all jacked up. When that stuff hits the fan, yeah, no problem, I've got this and all, ya know. Whatever the circumstance, everything clicks. Bird bouncing around, gear flying everywhere, alarms going off…you know how it is. I love it. Then I get back, and just standing in the checkout line to buy these beers is like, I lose it. It's stupid. It's loser stuff. We're better than that. I just don't know why I can't get my stuff together. I'm blowing it with Cynthia. I kicked the crap out of you."

"Whoa there, buddy. You were lucky you ran off when you did."

"And that's another thing. I've never run from a fight in my life. But I ran, and ran till I just lost it. I was kneeling on the dirty floor of this grocery store and looking at all this stuff we have here, and I thought about over there where those people have jack. Bombs blowing up all the time. It dawned on me that I had finally run from a fight. I hated myself. Still do, kinda." Jake paused. Aiden kept listening, so he continued.

"I got up and thought, how pathetic. What if the guys could see me now? I'm pissed at whatever this is. I want to beat it. That's what I told Cynthia. She said you can help and I know she's right." He paused again. "I'm sorry for being a moron. Sorry for all this."

Aiden took a long sip of his beer and looked at the ceiling. "I'm sorry, too. Now, I don't know how much time we have before you get your next assignment, I can't help you at all with Cynthia because I don't know a thing about being married, and I don't have any magic twelve steps to follow. Everyone is different. What's it going to take for you to defeat this? Couldn't tell ya. Will it ever go fully away? Probably not. But we can use it, and let the experiences grow us instead of own us. It's like so many other things in life – how bad do you want it?"

"I'm all in. How do we start?"

"Just like everything else, work your ass off. But can we wait and get started on Monday? I just want to get to bed."

PART III

14

Actionable

Al Hasakah, Syria 2008

Adnan Al-Kuli walked the same route he had walked every day for three weeks. He was beginning to tell who the regulars were: street merchants, business owners, thugs, and those in charge he didn't want to mess with. His focus was to keep his eyes open and look for people who didn't belong: foreigners and professionals. They normally stood out if you knew what to look for, and Adnan was well instructed. The third largest city in Syria had plenty of strangers coming and going, and the men he worked for wanted to know when one showed up. What they did with them after that was anybody's guess, but they never came back. They paid him, and that was enough.

Adnan moved across the street toward his favorite internet cafe. It wasn't his favorite because of the fare; rather, it was always busy, and busy places drew new faces, opportunities for him to watch and discover. He went to what was becoming his customary station in the corner near the front window so he could see most of the room. His screen faced the window, which was fine with him because he didn't care who looked at it. He did a quick search for computer parts and let the page load, then slowly began scrolling as he took chance glances around the room. Every time a new patron walked in the door, he took the opportunity to search the faces. By now he was an expert, and old men like him were mostly ignored by the young anyway.

After twenty minutes, he got ready to leave. There was nothing new today. He would move down the street to another location, and another after that, until it got too dark or until the 6:00pm call to prayer sounded. There were always more faces there.

Just as he was getting up, the door opened and two bearded men walked in. They were new and they had a look Adnan recognized instantly. He sat back down and became invisible again; he was just another nobody. The men's actions were predictable and they followed the pattern to the letter: They went straight to the most isolated terminal in the café, one sat and began typing while his companion sat next to him and scanned the room.

Amateurs, Adnan Al-Kuli thought.

The duo never noticed Adnan, who got up and left his terminal, walked out to the street, crossed it, and looked for their vehicle. He spotted it instantly. Either they were novices or they didn't care if they were noticed. Adnan took out his cell phone and held it backwards with his left hand. He dropped his arm by his side casually, turned and ordered food from a street vendor while simultaneously clicking pictures of the car behind him with his thumb. To any onlooker it would seem he was just holding his phone. When he got his food, he walked to a spot facing the vehicle's front, three spaces away. He pretended to dial, and then pretended to be arguing with someone on the other line as he chewed.

He was three bites in when the men emerged from the café, made a brisk trot to the vehicle, and drove away. Adnan saw their faces clearly as he yelled at his phone. They never saw him. He dialed a real number, and before the car was off the street several individuals were discussing what to do with its occupants, and with Adnan Al-Kuli.

Baghdad

The intelligence officer examined the computer map on his screen with a dozen red bubble pins marking locations both in and outside of Iraq: Shiraz and Tabriz in Iran, more in Pakistan and Saudi Arabia, and a large cluster of eight in or around Baghdad. The most recent pointed to an internet cafe in Al Hasakah, Syria. This one garnered the most attention, not because it was new, but because there was actionable intelligence along with it. Each pin indicated the location of a computer recently used to log onto an email account. The computers themselves were irrelevant, and the username itself was also fairly unimportant. What mattered was how frequently the username and password appeared, and in the variety of locations it did so, especially in certain areas of concern.

The wars in Afghanistan and Iraq were marvels of technology, and both sides knew how to use it not only on the battlefield, but in the small rooms and caves of its planners and on the vastness of the internet. Coalition forces were well aware from the beginning that they were dealing with a new level of sophistication on the part of their enemies. Whatever advantages America enjoyed in 2001 as a result of its technology were all too often skirted by the enemy's rapid adaptation. By 2004, the insurgents created weapons and systems of communication that forced Coalition intelligence services worldwide to come up with new infiltration methods.

Cell phones were both a nightmare and a blessing. When their prevalence reached new heights the world over by the mid-2000s, the Middle East was no exception; terrorists had cell phones just like everyone else did. Initially, the signals intelligence analysts had a field day with phone intercepts. American special operators or CIA field agents occasionally located a phone in a raid or on reconnaissance, and if opportunity struck, in a manner of seconds an American operator could remove a phone's SIM card, place it into a hand-held reader, and replace it without its owner being the wiser.

Later, everything that phone did would be an open book. But the terrorists adapted again, and started utilizing other methods. Email seemed a good method at first, but emails travel through servers, which were infiltrated and exploited. The cat and mouse game between the two sides continued.

The common nature of email clients afforded terrorist cells another tactic: the use of a single shared account. The terrorist cell's members would create an account and password and share it. The men communicated by logging onto the email account from wherever they were. A user would start composing a draft email, but wouldn't send it, leaving the text on the account under the 'Drafts' file until the other members received the message. It would then be deleted, amended, or responded to, again as a draft. In this manner, multiple cell members communicated with one another from all over the world without ever sending a message, or speaking or meeting in person. But Americans adapted as well, and with clever mathematics, were on to them again.

The map on the computer screen was working the problem. Programmers developed a series of algorithms that monitored the frequency of usernames, login combinations, and the locations of access. Computers cross-referenced that data with known or likely terrorist havens across the globe and plotted the trends automatically, alerting analysts when they peaked.

Soon the picture filled itself in, as it was doing now. This particular cell was already in play, their communications monitored for well over a month. But today was different. This time the username and password positively linked to a face many people were happy to see: Saeed Al-Maquatti.

Several individuals were already associated with the account, and American operators conducted raids on some of the ones residing in Iraq. Others they were still monitoring, waiting for additional connections, studying the patterns of communication and supply. The man spotted today in Syria,

Saeed Al-Maquatti, was way up the terrorist food chain.

Important terrorist leaders were killed or captured routinely, and Al-Maquatti emerged on the scene to fill the void. He was known to intelligence services as SAM, or Uncle Sam, as the field agents sometimes called him. He was an American-educated finance manager, funneling payments to insurgents by methods not entirely known. He had a degree of ownership in legitimate businesses in Yemen, Syria, and elsewhere, but rarely showed himself. It was believed that he used the accounting of various businesses to transfer and wash debts as payment for other "services" with other businesses in Iran and elsewhere. What was known was that he was smart, elusive, and deadly.

The recent email exchanges positively linked him to several attacks, and his number was up. But since then he had only been spotted once in Jordan, and the attempt to capture or kill him ended in a lot of dead bodies. Just not his.

Today, a combination of satellites tracked the vehicle through the streets of one of Syria's largest cities. In Iraq it would have been a simple matter of launching an assault; there were already two task forces, a combination of SEALs, Army Rangers, and other special operations assets dedicated to that purpose. They were veritable all-star teams, the best the world's elite military and intelligence services could provide, and they conducted raids almost every day in different sectors.

Years of keeping a force on standby waiting for Osama bin Laden to appear had weighed on the enthusiasm of the operators, and they were like attack dogs pulling against their chains, desperate to get into the action. They were antsy and frustrated, so the military brass decided to cut them loose and use their skills while always keeping an eye out, waiting for the big fish.

But big fish traveled, and cross-border operations were tricky. The politics could be complicated if SAM wasn't captured easily. Killing him and confiscating his computers was a much easier option, but in the middle of the city it would have to be accomplished with secrecy and finesse.

The other option was to get as close to him as possible and tag everything he owned. Tracking him and his network might prove incalculably more valuable than playing with his computers or seeing him in a body bag. Hundreds of people, from those in comfortable chairs in swank offices to those sleeping on dirty pallets sniffing in diesel fuel, all waited on the decision of what to do with Saeed Al-Maquatti.

Mosul, Iraq

Jake clicked Send and closed the laptop. He hardly knew any of the men around him. For what seemed like the hundredth time in his life, he was a new guy in a room full of veterans. Part of him felt ridiculous and out of place; another part felt right at home.

He was getting used to new tactics and learning lessons every day, but rarely of the medical variety. On each of his previous deployments, he had spent the lion's share of his time treating injuries and saving lives. Nowadays, he treated minor things like lacerations, IVs for dehydration, or the occasional broken bone, but he knew it was just a matter of time.

Two days earlier, a sniper took down an insurgent as he tried to set an IED. Through his scope, the sniper had watched the man crawl as he bled, expecting him to fall over any second, but thirty minutes later he was still rolling around in the dirty street.

It was a clean shooting, but they couldn't just leave him there all day.

"Take a medic out there and see what you can do about him," the lieutenant in charge had told the sniper. "And next time, if you're gonna shoot him, make sure you kill him."

The frustrated sniper called Jake over.

"Come on, let's see what you can do about that guy."

Jake led a squad out to the man in the street. As soon as he knelt over him, rifle fire erupted from an adjacent building. Jake never flinched. The squad assaulted the shooter's position, leaving Jake with the patient.

When they got back to Jake a few minutes later, he had the grateful man's wound packed and was ready to move him. The medics, corpsman, and their commanders began to take notice of the PJ's skill and equanimity under fire.

Jake was excited and a little bit scared when they assigned him to one of the special task forces in Iraq conducting mixed unit operations. Becoming a Navy SEAL had been his goal throughout his senior year of high school; he'd never even heard about Pararescue until Aiden joined the Air Force and started on that path. He loved being a PJ but part of him always wondered if he might have liked being a SEAL more. Now here he was, going on raids and getting into and out of scrapes with the best. Members of the Naval Special Warfare Development Group worked alongside Army Delta, CIA Special Activities Division, and Special Operations Group, as well as Ranger veterans from places Jake had never even heard of.

He felt very small. He loved it.

Every day was filled with things new to him and he was stretched way beyond his comfort zone. It was a perfect challenge. Since he didn't have to partake in any of the mission planning and leaders were asking for him by name, the action was constant. He went from one op to the next, rarely sleeping in a bunk, stealing cat naps whenever he could. But he didn't long for sleep; in fact, he wanted more missions. It was hard to explain to Cynthia, or even Hector, but everything about it gelled. Yet he still wondered why he was here.

The SEALs had their own version of medic called corpsman. Jake knew they trained in Navy and civilian hospitals and were every bit as skilled in battlefield emergencies as PJs, and at first he worried they might resent his assignment.

But they didn't. The corpsmen were confident, competent, and deeply grateful for Jake's contribution. They weren't medical SEALs, but they were SEALs who knew medicine, and Jake freed them up to be assaulters, primarily. They preferred making holes to patching them, and having Jake and the other PJs in the task force meant they could sublet the purple glove work and be in on more of the action.

For their part, the Army had plenty of medics around, but with the increase in attacks and the sophistication of insurgent destructive capabilities, greater assessment skill and care were needed. They were in the early stages of creating a top-shelf medical training program, but for now they knew that beyond the first responder stage, their medics couldn't compete with PJs. Task force commanders wanted the best care available for their men, guys who could practically perform surgery in a firefight if necessary, who could also do everything asked of them operationally on land, on sea, or in the air. They wanted PJs, and Jake was among the best the Air Force had.

From the moment he landed, he was on the move. Every deployment was unique in its own way, but Jake had never experienced anything like this. Despite being there for months, he'd had few personal conversations; the commanders were enforcing a new level of operational ferocity and there was hardly any time to email his wife, much less make friends.

Jake sat, relieved he'd managed to get a message off to Cynthia. He thought about attempting to get some sleep but wasn't tired, which was fine because he sensed something was up. He decided to get something to eat and then maybe check his gear for the hundredth time. He didn't want to let any of these guys down, or himself.

Pope Field, North Carolina

Cynthia reread the email three times before she hit the print button. It was so short, she savored every word.

She understood the nature of his new assignment and was grateful Jake managed to send her notes whenever he could.

She didn't worry about him. There was a new level of connection and a feeling of peace she had a hard time describing. She wasn't immune to the chill of fear, but it didn't own her. She loved her husband and wanted him doing what he was designed for: saving lives. She was on his side, and Jake knew it.

Cynthia was a new girl in a strange town with no real friends, and living on the east coast in an entirely new environment was strange. After emerging from the culture shock she fell in love with the south. The food was amazing. Cynthia had never experienced barbecue like this; she felt she could eat a whole hog every day and not be sorry for it.

Cynthia took the page off the printer, folded it, and put it next to all the others in the drawer. She walked to the bathroom and paused in front of the mirror, almost two dozen pastel sticky notes with Jake's handwriting adhered to it. Cynthia turned around and looked at herself from different angles, running her hand over her belly and decided she could justify another night of pulled pork, and maybe some ice cream. She smiled. *He'll be home soon enough.*

15

Adnan Al-Kuli

Al Hasakah, Syria

Adnan Al-Kuli sat on a bed reading a book he had no interest in. It was a cheap manual on understanding and writing computer code. He had a degree in communications networking from Oxford University — or so his cover story went — and traveled as an information technology specialist. Adnan was operating in Syria as a Jordanian according to his current passport.

His real name was Dominic Reyes, who, for the better part of his sixty years, was a CIA field agent. Puerto Rican by heritage, he didn't speak a word of Spanish growing up in 1950s Pennsylvania. Dominic was smart, creative, and an incredibly fast learner who turned heads in school and later in the Marine Corps with his ability to adapt under pressure. The ink on his discharge form was still wet when the CIA came calling to recruit Reyes into his second career.

After thirty-seven years of service — first in Cuba, but eventually all across the globe — he spoke eight languages fluently, and had burned through three times as many cover identities and one marriage. For the last three years he primarily had spoken Arabic, which was not a problem, but he was spending hours every day struggling to learn a new language: computers.

As Dominic studied the book, he knew it was only a matter of minutes before a text message for Adnan would have him on the road again, and it was entirely probable computers would not factor into his next mission in the slightest.

"So the little *less than* sign goes before what you want to see on the screen, and you put another little *greater than* sign after it," Dominic said in Arabic.

"Right. Think of it as a door, maybe. You open it, give the command, and then close it," his younger partner answered, also in Arabic.

"So anything inside the signs will show up on the screen?"

"Correct."

"I will master you, foolish machine," Dominic said.

"I'm calling you Neo from now on."

"Who?"

"It's from a movie. He could dodge bullets, ya know."

"That might be helpful."

Amer Fahri was about thirty years his junior, and known as Jessie in another world. Amer's cover was that of a Palestinian from Israel, also Oxford-trained and working for the same computer company, but with considerably more knowledge of coding. He knew computers far better than Dominic – but on everything else he listened, followed, and learned every lesson Dominic was willing to teach him. Not a day passed when Dominic didn't teach Jessie something that could save both their lives.

Jessie was new to the CIA, but not to war. He was a former SEAL due to a torn Achilles tendon that never fully healed, resulting in a slight limp and occasional pain despite the injury being a decade old. After getting reassigned as diplomatic security in Venezuela in 2000, he had made friends with CIA field personnel. Then the war started.

Like Dominic, he also had language skills, but more importantly, Jessie also looked the part. Either of them could walk into any cafe in the Middle East without turning heads. They operated as a team, but were rarely seen together.

In 2005 it was clear the insurgency in Iraq was being fueled from neighboring countries. Men and women like Dominic and Jessie were constantly circling Iraq's periphery, collecting intelligence, tracking sources, setting up data collection networks, and eliminating targets.

Jessie's laptop chimed with a new email. Dominic put down his book and moved to read it over his shoulder, then pulled out a rugged tablet. The durable hand-held device was fed maps, routes, buildings, and highway information. In a few minutes, Dominic familiarized himself with the street and the target building while Jessie gathered their gear, which was minimal. They traveled light with nondescript black carry-on bags, each filled with clothes just like every other businessman in the world. Dominic had an attaché case for the laptop and tablet; Jessie had a small but heavy backpack.

Ten minutes after receiving the initial email, the CIA operatives walked out the door of the rented apartment they'd never set foot in again, and into the dark street. They put the carry-on bags in the trunk and everything else in the back seat of what appeared to be a rental car, but under the plain exterior it was a 2000 Ford SVT Mustang Cobra R, with one of Ford's most powerful engines.

Dominic had run across it three weeks ago, wrecked in Damascus. He dropped CIA cash to buy the scrapped vehicle and paid twice as much to make it look like a run-of-the-mill rental car, with new body components but all of the 385hp V8 engine. He knew the day would probably come when he'd need to get out of Syria in a hurry.

Jessie drove and Dominic leaned back in the passenger seat and closed his eyes. It was at least an hour's drive, and Adnan Al-Kuli was well aware this might be his only chance to sleep for quite some time. But first they needed to pick up one more piece of luggage.

—

Mosul, Iraq

"How long now?"

"They've been parked for almost three hours, sir."

"No others?"

"Negative. We're tracking a few vehicles moving along the highway, mainly large fuel trucks and tractor trailers. It's all quiet."

General Dawson, the task force commander, was frustrated. As soon as Saeed Al-Maquatti's vehicle started driving outside the city, he wanted to take it out. He was told to stand by for authorization.

He waited. Men and women at computer screens waited. Drone operators waited with fingers on the trigger. The SUV stopped briefly on the outskirts of the city and was joined by two others. SAM was again positively identified from the air. There was no doubt. One of the most wanted terrorists on the list was leisurely rolling down a largely empty highway.

It was the easiest target Dawson had ever seen, but it drove unmolested for more than an hour. A younger Dawson would have screamed, but by now he was too familiar with the bureaucracy of war. Politics were always the enemy of action, and he understood that both had their place. Still, it was a juicy opportunity, and he didn't want it to get away.

The three-vehicle caravan eventually moved into a small petrol industrial area where they separated. It caused a mild panic, as people behind computer screens scrambled to watch the SUV shell game, trying to confirm the one that contained SAM while not losing the other two. They breathed a sigh of relief when all three parked, albeit approximately five miles apart.

They had SAM — and whoever was traveling with him — in their crosshairs. It was a tight spot. If they destroyed the vehicle with a bomb, it likely would ignite a fire that could destroy the adjacent petrol facilities with civilian casualties. It would certainly make news, so it was a bad option, which is why Dawson was frustrated. They could have taken out all three vehicles on the road hours ago, and nobody would have cared except a few truck drivers forced to detour around the flames. Now, things were complicated.

Dawson planned to attack the vehicles if they could get a clear shot, if they moved again outside the city, but the drones couldn't circle in Syrian airspace indefinitely without detection. He wanted them to get back on the road; unfortunately, they were just sitting there. The cameras caught SAM and three men walking into the building they were parked next to, and everyone was still inside. It could be hours, or even days, before they moved. Or they could move on foot and leave the vehicles parked where they were. Dawson's next plan was to unleash the task force into Syria and breech the building. He had staffers working on an assault plan, but suddenly he got word from higher up that someone had come up with another option, and it was already in motion.

Al Hasakah, Syria

Jessie pulled over and parked on the curb. "You awake?" he asked.

"No. Make it snappy."

Jessie got out and walked into the hotel lobby with his backpack. He immediately took the staircase to the second floor and found the appropriate room. He took a breath, then opened the door.

Inside the room, a woman in western dress sat on the bed in bare feet, typing on a laptop. She took no notice of him and merely pointed to a chair in the corner, never taking her eyes off the screen. Jessie slowly turned his head and saw a man standing behind the door holding a lowered pistol. He didn't look at Jessie, either.

Jessie walked to the chair and picked up the white plastic bag, turned, and walked back out of the room without speaking to or making eye contact with either of its occupants . He scanned the dark hallway, but the hotel was practically deserted. It was eerie. Even the desk clerk seemed like an uninterested prop.

Back at the car, Jessie handed the bag to Dominic, who took it while still pretending to sleep. Dominic waited until they were heading south on the highway and then opened the bag, pulling out two Styrofoam food containers. He opened them and began assembling the radio and headset combinations within. He set the radio and the earpiece on himself and then on Jessie as he drove. When they were situated comfortably, Dominic sat back into his seat and closed his eyes before speaking into the radio.

"Marathon One, ETA to target Alpha, sixty-three minutes." And then Adnan Al-Kuli truly went to sleep; he knew he would need it. The kid could do the talking.

—

Mosul, Iraq

"Marathon is coming up now. ETA ten minutes."

General Dawson watched the small car descend into the frame, moving slowly along the highway. Just before it exited, the driver turned off its headlights.

—

Ash Shaddadi, Syria

Jessie pulled the car to a slow stop in the shadow of an abandoned building, two blocks from their objective. They were going to walk to it; they already had the approach memorized. Jessie slung his backpack over his shoulder, and Dominic put his attaché case containing the computer and tablet in the trunk. Few of the buildings had exterior lights and most of the windows along the street were dark.

"Marathon Two in position."

"Copy, Marathon, we have visual. Proceed on foot to objective Alpha."

Dominic's hands were free. A cell phone was in his left front pocket, cash and his Jordanian passport in his right. For weapons, he had two police-style stun grenades and two fragmentation grenades in his jacket's inside pocket, and a pistol with five magazines on the small of his back. Walking down the street, he looked like any other sixty-year-old, slightly overweight Syrian. Jessie too had a pistol, but his backpack also contained door breech explosives and a Heckler and Koch UMP submachine gun with a folding stock and six magazines, containing twenty-five .45 caliber rounds each. He also had med kit essentials in his back pockets.

If they encountered anyone on the walk, Dominic planned to say they were almost out of gas and needed directions to a fuel station. He hoped he wouldn't have to kill anyone, even SAM, and instead would be able to hand him over in a quiet meeting in the desert with people on the other end of the radio.

The street was quiet. Jessie tried to avoid looking at all of the rooftops but had an aching sensation that eyes were watching his every move. Against his instinct he took his cues from Dominic, who strolled like he was on his way to pick up a bagel on Sunday morning. They were being watched closely, but not by Syrian locals. American reconnaissance satellites followed every step, and an assortment of air assets monitored communications between Marathon and task force head-quarters.

Dominic recognized the vehicle before he recognized the building; it was the same SUV he had spotted earlier in the day. He had hoped to catch SAM within the vehicle, perhaps on the road, even. He frowned when he saw it was empty, and knew he had to rely on intel from above that said their target was in the building. So many times in his career the intel was wrong, but there was nothing to do about it. Dominic walked around the SUV, looking into the windows to confirm no driver; most of the windows were tinted. Jessie kept an eye on the vehicle and backed up to the building. He was holding his pistol inside his jacket pocket.

If all went well, he would only need a few zip ties. He went up to the door and gently pushed on it. When it didn't move, he decided to try the handle, but it was locked. Sometimes entry was much easier than expected; it was surprising how many people left their doors unlocked.

Now he had a decision to make. He could do a soft knock, which meant simply knocking on the door and seeing who answered. This would play into their cover story, but it would also eliminate the element of surprise. Dominic knew anyone answering this door would be doing so armed and ready to kill. But he also knew he could easily dispatch several men before the first hit the ground, if necessary. Option two would be to breech the door forcibly, either by kicking it in or with explosives, which would alert more than just the building's occupants.

He decided to knock.

Dominic knocked on the door three times. Then he put his hands in his pockets and took a step back. He lowered his eyes and waited, and prayed. To anyone inside, he appeared nonthreatening.

There was no answer.

After a minute, he knocked again.

He prayed sweat didn't appear on his forehead, as his heart began beating faster. Jessie stood still, back against the building, eyes looking ahead but focused on the periphery. After two minutes, Dominic considered walking away, perhaps waiting for them to get back in the vehicles. But before he turned to look at Jessie, the door cracked open.

"What do you want?" a man said, not bothering to open the door wide enough to be seen from the outside.

Four decades of field experience took over and in an instant Dominic decided his best play. He kicked in the door, pulled out his pistol, and put a bullet in the head of the man as he was falling backward. Dominic cleared the entryway expertly and was already walking to the next room before Jessie was inside. Lights were on and it was easy to see the small building was practically empty, and quiet. *The wrong building? Bad intel?* Dominic began to fear he'd just killed an innocent man.

There was still one room at the end of the hall; the door was cracked and lights were on inside. Jessie took a knee and aimed at the door while Dominic crept toward it. He paused against the wall a foot away, pulled out one of the non-lethal flashbang grenades, and tossed it inside.

The stun grenade was filled with a pyrotechnic metal-oxidant mix of magnesium and potassium nitrate. When it detonated, it produced a blinding light that assaulted the optic nerves of the men in the room and generated a percussion that created inner-ear trauma to disorient them. The effects took most people at least five seconds to begin shaking off. It was more than Dominic needed.

When the explosion of light and noise erupted, Dominic opened the door and Jessie aimed inside while walking toward it. Jessie saw two men holding AK-47s, eyes closed and struggling to not fall over. Jessie made a quick scan of their faces and recognized the one he'd been studying for months. He aimed at the other one, and put three shots into his chest.

Dominic kicked the legs out from under Saeed Al-Maquatti, put his foot down hard on the terrorist's forearm, and planted his knee into his back. He then shoved his head into the floor, breaking his nose, then pulled his hands behind his back. The violence was so spectacularly efficient that SAM had no way to respond. Jessie flex-cuffed his wrists before the man's eyesight had even corrected.

Dominic performed a hasty check for other weapons but didn't see any. They saw a laptop on the desk was turned on and a phone on the floor; Jessie grabbed both and held them under his arm as he helped Dominic pull the terrorist to his feet. The two-man team was about to rush him out the door to the when they heard a warning in their earpieces.

"Marathon, we have armed hostiles exiting objective Bravo."

Now it was clear to Jessie and Dominic. After hearing the first shot — maybe after the first knock — Saeed's bodyguard must have told his master to be still while they called in backup from down the street. Who knew how many of his entourage were on their way?

"Grab him, and let's move," Dominic said.

Jessie holstered his pistol. They had to drag Saeed out as his legs were still wobbly. When they got to the still-open front door, Dominic threw him to the ground. Jessie knelt next to him and put his pistol barrel inches from his head. Dominic took a quick glance out the door. The street was still dark, but he heard vehicles approaching.

———

Mosul, Iraq

Several eyes were watching the dual SUVs outside objective Bravo while Marathon conducted the raid down the street.

Two additional vehicles were parked outside Bravo and occasionally a straggler walked out of the building. As soon as Marathon One kicked in the door at Alpha, the analysts saw movement at Bravo. Lights in the building went out, but the infrared picked up two men moving to the windows. They were not there long. Before the flashbang went off, six heavily armed men rushed out the door and climbed into the two SUVs. As they pulled away, more men were seen exiting the building into additional vehicles.

"Two vehicles moving at a high rate of speed toward objective Alpha."

There was little the overhead surveillance could do but watch and warn, and prepare for whatever the two Marathon operatives decided to do next. General Dawkins knew this could get ugly fast. He reached over and picked up a phone.

———

Ash Shaddadi, Syria

Another thirty seconds and they could have disappeared into the shadows of the street, but the oncoming headlights were pointing straight at the building entrance. Dominic looked away, holstered his pistol and pulled out one of the two grenades from inside his jacket. He repositioned to get the parked SUV between him and the headlights, and knelt beside the rear wheel. His knee was immediately sore. His body felt the effects of constant tension, physical challenges, and little sleep, and he rarely got time to work out like he did when he was younger. If they had to make a run for it, he'd have a hard time keeping pace with Jessie. He'd need to rely on firepower to get out of this, which he didn't have.

But Jessie did. Some, anyway.

While Dominic took up a position beside the SUV, Jessie knelt on Saeed in the doorway and opened his backpack. He pulled out the submachine gun and unfolded the stock, inserted a magazine and readied it, waiting.

He wasn't sure what Dominic was going to do.

The first vehicle slowed, and Jessie could see four people through the lowered windows. He couldn't see Dominic on the other side of the SUV, but he would wait for him to make the first move.

Dominic stood and pulled the pin on the grenade. He was going to wait until the vehicle parked to toss it, but he noticed the driver had his window down. He decided to lob it into the open window instead.

A lifetime of throwing grenades in combat, in training, and in the field gave him the confidence and skill to toss it underhand, slow-pitch softball style into the moving vehicle. The grenade actually hit the driver in the chin, fell to the floorboard and exploded as the front seat passengers looked at it in confusion. The explosion devoured most of the lower bodies of the front passengers and a significant amount of the rear occupants. Dominic stepped around the SUV and shot what was left of the driver's chest, then put two bullets into the rear passengers as the vehicle idled past him and into the side of the building.

The second SUV braked hard and stopped ten feet behind it. Jessie stood up and put a line of bullets into the distorted hulk of the first vehicle, aimed and fired into the windshield of the second until the magazine was spent, then paused to change it.

Dominic was at his side now and looked at Saeed Al-Maquatti lying face down on the ground, spent bullet casings all around him. He looked up and saw injured men pouring out of the back of the second SUV as Jessie leveled his weapon and finished them off with his second magazine.

They heard another vehicle approaching, and Dominic had another decision to make.

Saeed was a treasure trove of information, but the op to capture and interrogate him was a wash. As much as Dominic's colleagues would have loved to mine the terrorist for all he was worth, it simply wasn't possible now. Given the opportunity, they might even have been willing to strike a deal and pay him for cooperation. Dominic wished for one hour alone with Saeed; he knew he could have gotten something valuable.

But none of that mattered. Their vehicle was two blocks away, and bad guys were regrouping and reinforcing. He and Jessie would be lucky to escape alive. He also couldn't afford to let SAM slip away. He didn't like it, he never liked it. He never enjoyed killing anything, even animals, but so many times he had to. He wished tonight had gone more smoothly, but in his experience things rarely went smoothly. *We have his phone and computer at least, if we can get them out of here.* He didn't have an option.

Dominic kicked Saeed over and looked directly at the face of one of many men responsible for so much death in Iraq and elsewhere. Dominic made a mental identification in case he ever got the chance to give another debriefing, pointed his pistol in Saeed's chest, and pulled the trigger three times.

Jessie never looked. He knew it was the best bad option.

"We need to move," he said.

"Back to the car, double back, this way," Dominic said and turned to trot down the street perpendicular to the one they were parked on two blocks north. Jessie moved backward firing short bursts and noticed two additional sets of head-lights. He turned to follow Dominic, who was running to the end of the block. The CIA operatives moved in the shadows, but shadows were disappearing rapidly as the explosions woke the town. People were looking out windows, and Dominic and Jessie heard voices all around them.

At the end of each block, Dominic stopped, looked around the corner, and ran again. Jessie was right behind him, easily closing the distance with the older man. In the two hours since Dominic first saw this street's layout on the digital map, he had planned this alternate escape route and he recognized the landmarks.

"This is it. It's on this one," he said, huffing.

Jessie peeked around the corner and saw their rental car at the end of the block. There were lights on all around; a few people were in the street looking for the drama source. Dominic walked the remaining distance trying to look casual. Jessie was behind him trying unsuccessfully to conceal the machine gun under his jacket. Onlookers stared at the unfamiliar man with the moustache, and Dominic shot some of them a look that said *Go away.* Jessie was ready to shoot anyone with a weapon, but nobody was armed.

They reached the car and heard the approach of vehicles and many voices calling out as they opened the doors. Two military-aged men pointed at them, shouting.

Dominic started the engine and gunned the gas, pulling away with screeching tires. Jessie reclined the passenger seat as far as it would go and turned around to figure out which window he might need to fire out of. He saw three vehicles out the rear window, closing fast: two mid-sized trucks and another black SUV. Men hung out of the SUV windows, and more men were in the backs of the trucks.

Dominic accelerated to 80mph, but had to brake to avoid road obstacles, then pressed the pedal again trying to find his way back onto the highway. He pulled up the map in his head and remembered the right road, pulling the wheel hard to the left as Jessie struggled to keep his balance inside the small car. The driver side door was briefly exposed to the oncoming vehicles.

The nearest truck had four men with AK-47 rifles in the back and one in the passenger seat. When they saw the clear shot of the side of the car they unloaded their weapons at it. Not all of the one hundred and fifty bullets fired hit the car, but enough did to riddle the metal frame and shatter all of the left side glass, along with much of Dominic as well. But even with bullets passing through his body he managed to keep his foot on the gas.

Jessie and Dominic bled from several wounds, and Dominic's arms fell from the wheel. The car started to veer off the road, and Jessie dropped his weapon and grabbed the steering wheel. They were bumping along on the highway approaching 100mph and Jessie struggled to keep them on the road and straight.

"Keep on the gas, Dom," he said in English, for the first time in months.

"This is Marathon Two, we could use some help here! You're seeing this, right?"

"Copy Marathon. Maintain your current course," a calm voice said into their earpieces. Jessie looked over his shoulder. Now there were lights from four vehicles behind them.

16

Razor

Sinjar, Northern Iraq

The battering ram slammed into the door and sent an echo down the dark street like a wave. Jake thought it would wake the entire town. It didn't matter; the breach was complete, and he followed four men into the dark house. The illumination through his night vision gave a hazy green glow, but it was still clearer than any he'd ever used. This unit got the best gear on the market, and the difference was immense.

At the same time the five men breached from the street level, another four men had dropped out the side doors of an AH-6M Little Bird onto the roof. A second Little Bird, fitted with Hellfire anti-tank missiles, 7.62 miniguns, MK19 grenade launchers, and 50 caliber gun pods, buzzed around the building providing gunship cover.

It was known to some as the Killer Egg, a terror of the night sky, and Ed Tanner, piloting Star Four, adored his. Its wings were loaded with weapons and had yet to fire a round tonight.

The Little Birds were light, fast, and able to land anywhere their aggressive pilots were willing to go — in this case, onto a small roof in a densely-populated, dangerous town. They were part of the Special Operation Aviation Regiment — SOAR —better known as Night Stalkers, and arguably the best in the world.

Hovering high overhead were two Night Stalker Blackhawks, waiting out of range of ground fire for the order to pick up any cargo the assaulting team might find inside.

The street-level team rushed to clear the first floor while the roof team cleared the second. Jake heard the metallic action from two shots out of the lead man's suppressed rifle, then saw him back out of that room, and the procession kept moving.

Jake stopped in the doorway and glanced in. Two figures were face down, a pool of blood growing beneath them. They would clearly bleed out if they weren't already dead. Their hands were outstretched above them, a rifle not far away. The PJ in Jake wondered if he could revive them, but he knew he would just have to watch them bleed. It went against every instinct he had but he also knew there was much more at stake. The individuals on the ground clearly had intended to kill, and it had sealed their fate.

"First level clear," Jake heard over the radio.

He heard boots stomping on the floor above him, doors getting kicked in. There were other sounds, close-quarters violence that Jake was beginning to recognize and get comfortable with. It was all over in less than a minute.

"Second level clear. Get up here."

"Copy that," the first-level leader said. He turned to Jake and the man next to him. "Check them out and gather any intel. Watch for booby traps."

"Roger that," they said.

The first-level leader and another operative moved to the staircase at the end of the hall.

Jake took slow, deliberate steps toward the dying. He took off his night vision and turned the bedroom lights on. There were few furnishings and little in the way of intel — no computers, no file cabinets — just a bed, a man on the ground, and a dead or dying woman next to him. Jake kicked gently at the man's leg to see if there was any sign of life. There wasn't; he was gone, they both were.

The other American picked up the back of the man's jacket. "Whew," he whistled. "This Muj is loaded."

Jake looked and saw the man was wearing several bars of explosives in a vest. He probably could have taken out everyone on both floors. Something caused him to hesitate just long enough for the Americans to get the drop on him, sparing the lives of nine men. It was so random. *So lucky?* He hated the reality that men like this existed, that they taught children to do the same. He hated this war, hated that but for the split-second decision to pull a single trigger, Cynthia and eight others would have been widows. He thought about the men on the second floor, Americans and Iraqis. Jake wondered what was going on upstairs when his radio chimed.

"If those two are dead, get up here. We need to roll."

"Copy that," Jake said.

They ran up the staircase and saw one of the second-level guys with his gun on three men, flex-cuffed and lying face down. Three more Americans moved in and out of two rooms, filling trash bags with anything of potential intelligence value, tossing in a variety of loose papers and books, along with a cheap camera and four or five VHS videotapes. There were also a number of cell phones and a few sticks of explosives and detonators that they secured in a more delicate manner.

"What's downstairs?" the second-level team leader asked Jake.

"Man and woman dead. Dude has a vest on loaded to blow. We left it alone. Everything else is secure."

"Roger that," the leader keyed the transmitter on his microphone. "Star One, we've got cargo. Exiting to the roof in three mikes."

"Copy that, Razor," a Blackhawk pilot replied. "Star Three, come in behind me. Star Four, maintain perimeter."

"Razor Seven, get your butts up to the roof or I'm leaving you here," he said to the two men watching the road from the building's front entrance.

"Copy that," Razors Seven and Eight said at the same time.

Jake helped haul one of the hog-tied prisoners to the roof. When he exited the building, one of the Blackhawks was already moving into a hover, kicking up dust all around. The prisoners were thrown into the open side door of the helicopter and six of the Razor operators jumped in after them.

The large Blackhawk moved away before the fourth operator was seated, abruptly changing direction and pulling up and out into the darkness. The rotor noise never diminished because the Star Three Little Bird rocketed in and spun in mid-air directly over the four remaining Americans and dropped to a perfect hover with its skids only inches above the roof. Its pilot worked the controls while the copilot checked to see all four men were on board.

"We're good, let's go," he told the pilot.

"Star Four, we're outta here," the pilot said.

"Right behind ya," the other Little Bird pilot answered. None of the four helicopters had fired a shot.

The Little Bird's door was just wide enough to accommodate two men sitting side by side. Jake was directly behind the pilot with Razor One next to him. Razors Seven and Eight were on the other side, their legs dangling as the helicopter made jerking movements to clear the town's electrical wiring and throw off anyone who might be trying to take aim at them. They were soon clear and moving across the black desert landscape, again in a zigzag trajectory with the other three helicopters. Jake closed his eyes, but the motion compelled him to keep them open. His heart beat slower as the adrenaline he had been swimming in for the past half hour receded. He was ready for a thirty-minute hop home.

"Star Two, say again, over?" Jake heard his pilot say through his earpiece.

Jake heard chatter but wasn't sure what to make of it. After a few seconds he felt his seat make another violent pitch up, then to the left. It gained speed, more speed than Jake was used to as it flew sideways. The helicopter leveled out much closer to the ground than Jake had ever experienced and gained even more speed as its tail rotor picked up, and it flew at an angle.

"Hang on boys, gonna pick up some milk on the way home," Jake heard the pilot say with a smile in his voice.

—

Eastern Syria

Jessie was shot, but thankfully not in his arms. He kept a firm grip on the left side of the steering wheel while watching the road but knew he would have to let go and start shooting eventually.

"Dom, you still with me, bro?"

"Affirmative." Speaking was difficult and painful.

Dominic could barely see the road through the broken windshield. Few cars were on the highway at this time of night, mainly large delivery trucks. He had been hit broadside and bullets had passed through his legs, thighs, side, and shoulders. Something — maybe a bullet, maybe glass — had skimmed his forehead, and blood was trickling into his eyes, thickening in the rush of air; most of the car windows were broken.

Jessie saw trucks in the rearview mirror, gaining on them. "They're coming up fast, Dom. I need you to get your hands on the wheel. Get your war on, bro."

Jessie reached into his back pocket, took what bandages he had, and rammed them into some of Dominic's wounds.

Dominic was close to passing out from the pain. He couldn't move the left side of his body, but his right side responded and he kept his foot on the gas. He couldn't see the speedometer. He blinked away the fluids around his eyes and tried to straighten himself in the seat. The pain made him see stars.

Get it together. Just one thing at a time. Grab the wheel.

Somehow he managed to bring his right arm up and replace Jessie's hand on the wheel. He got three fingers and his thumb as far as the five o'clock position, inverted on the steering wheel. "I got it," he said.

Jessie, seeing Dominic with a limp grasp, tried letting go. The car started to swerve but Dominic held it straight enough.

"Just keep straight on this road." Jessie turned his attention back to the rear, and lifted the machine gun.

"How many?" Dominic asked.

"Still four, I think, we've got some distance."

"Jess, what's that?" Dominic saw shapes and red lights in front of him.

Jessie turned and saw their car fast approaching the taillights of two tractor trailers.

"Brakes, Dom!"

Dominic pumped the brakes and Jessie was flung into the dashboard, almost out the broken windshield but for holding on to his seat's headrest. The car almost came to a stop.

"No, don't stop! Get around them, to the right."

Dominic could hardly see, much less steer. He pressed the accelerator and veered to the right of one of the trucks. Jessie retook the wheel. The small car bounced off the road managing to get mostly around the truck. Jessie looked back and saw the headlights following them around the big trucks. Jessie steered them back onto the road in front of the truck. Dominic retook the wheel, but the separation from their pursuers had all but vanished. They heard pinging and crunching sounds behind them as bullets hit the trunk and rear windshield, and Jessie.

He swore, raised the machine gun, and fired into the car behind him, causing it to swerve. He reloaded his third magazine.

"Dom, gas it up! Lose these guys!"

Dominic tried to look into the rearview mirror but it was pointless. Blood caked the side of his face; his left eye was barely open. He used all the energy he could muster and pressed his foot on the pedal. The car regained distance, but not for long.

A small projectile emitted from the bed of the truck closed the distance and streaked into the ground beneath their right rear wheel, jolting the car a few inches off the ground before the explosion. The wheels found the road in a violent impact, skidding as the tires touched down. The rear tire was on the rim, and the car thumped along for another mile at 80mph, then 70, then 60. The torn rubber and steel started smoking.

Jessie used the slowing speed to shoulder the machine gun and take several bursts at the windshield of the lead truck, which swerved and backed off by five car lengths. They were obviously aware that Dom and Jessie's car was dying and would soon have to pull over or crash. "We're gonna have to fight this out," Jessie said changing magazines again.

"Not sure I can move."

"Alright, here." Jessie pulled the seat belt over Dominic's lap and fastened it, then sat down and pulled on his own. There was glass all over his seat, cutting into his backside, blood mixing with gunshot wounds. "Drive us as far off the road into the dark as you can. When it slows enough, turn to the right and try to roll out the door. I'll cover you."

"So you want me to crash. Sure, why not?"

Jessie let his muscles relax to minimize damage on impact, all except for his grip on his weapon's handle.

Dominic steered the car off the road, into and over the sand at 40 mph. The car bounced several times until it became sluggish on the uneven ground about fifteen feet off the road. As instructed, Dominic pulled the wheel as hard as the working parts of his right hand would allow him to, and the car slowly rotated.

Jessie reached down to unbuckle Dom's seatbelt, and shoved open the driver side door for him.

"Get out Dom, and get down," Jessie said, aiming his gun at the lights of the truck in front of him. Jessie was in the spotlight of the four pursuing vehicles when they slowed and turned, branching out across both lanes and blocking the road.

Jessie sprayed the front of the first truck and the headlights exploded. Its doors opened as the other truck came around it to a screeching halt, followed by another, their drivers confused about how to attack the disabled car.

Jessie took his chance and jumped out after Dominic, landing on top of the older man who was lying on his bad side. Jessie pulled Dominic's pistol out of the holster and put it in Dom's hand.

"Left flank! Left flank!" Jessie said and pointed, then ran to the right.

From his vantage point under the front bumper, Dominic aimed and fired at the feet ten meters away. Jessie took a knee behind the right taillight and unloaded what remained in magazine number four. He quickly reloaded and began shooting single aimed shots at anything that moved, wishing for an M4 with a scope.

"Dom, how we look?"

Dominic wiped his eyes with the forearm of the hand holding the pistol, "They're pinned. More coming. Let loose, Jess."

Jessie let two short bursts fly, keenly aware he only had two more magazines, then he would be down to a pistol as well.

Dominic knew they must be low on ammo, and time. He set down his pistol, keyed his mic, "Marathon One …getting overrun…any help?"

17

Night Stalkers

Northern Iraq

"Star Three, Star Four, get low, get fast. I've got the lead. We need to haul." Gonzales was behind the controls of his Blackhawk.

"Roger that," the Little Bird pilots said.

"We've got a highway coming up. No traffic."

"Power lines at fifty feet, Star Two. Over or under?"

"Under, don't hit any vehicles."

"Or donkeys," Star Three's copilot said.

All six pilots smiled; they knew he was right.

As Star One took the prisoners back to their base, along with most of the Razor assault team, the three remaining Night Stalkers were directed onto a different mission. The three helicopters raced between five and ten feet off the ground. There were plenty of obstacles to hit as the terrain rose and fell, and one could never know what was out there in the dark.

The Little Birds followed the Blackhawk for two reasons: it had significantly more sophisticated navigational equipment, and it was much faster. The Blackhawk's cruise speed of 170 mph could technically be pushed up to 220mph, and Gonzales was getting there.

With only its two pilots and two crew chiefs on board, Star Two was light. Gonzales pushed the engines to max power, as fast as he'd ever driven the aircraft. He was familiar with the area after dozens of missions, but moving in a straight line was extremely dangerous – it gave ground enemies a chance to see them coming. He hoped the speed and low elevation would nullify at least that risk, but there were others.

There was always a balance between the safety of his aircrew and the mission. All he knew was that there were Americans on the ground getting overrun and that if he didn't get to them fast, this would merely be a recovery mission for dead bodies. He was a Night Stalker, and that was unacceptable.

Gonzales knew without asking that all twelve men on the three helicopters wanted to take the risk. He had no idea what to expect when they crossed the border, nor did he care. He was going to get there as fast as his machine would take them.

If flying the Blackhawk was akin to driving a luxury car, the Little Bird that Ed Tanner and his copilot Jordan followed him in was more akin to a small race car. It had less power and wasn't as comfortable, but it had greater agility.

They'd piloted the attack helicopter together for six years, but Ed had been flying much longer than that, cutting his teeth in east Africa in the 1990s and a dozen duty assignments since. He was also proficient with Blackhawks and Chinooks, and had distinguished himself in special operations around the globe. His first love was the Little Bird, and especially the AH-6M variant he was racing tonight.

Flying to Ed's right was an MH-6M, also a Little Bird, but with a difference. Star Three was configured for insertion and extraction. Its sides were fitted with benches for operators such as Jake and the other Razor team members to sit on. It had weapons too, but nothing like what Ed and Jordan had at their disposal.

"All clear," Gonzales said as the larger helicopter zipped under the power lines and across the empty highway.

"Right behind ya," Ed said. "Star Four clear."

"Star Three clear."

"Look out ahead, there's some livestock," Gonzales said. The Little Birds saw the Blackhawk bank to the left to avoid hitting what looked like a shepherd and a herd of goats.

"Roger, Star Two."

"I see 'em," Star Four said.

The Little Birds followed the Blackhawk's lead, using minor adjustments to avoid land obstacles illuminated by night vision. Gonzales banked right, then left, then pulled up sharply, then dropped into a wadi and pitched down, always hugging the surface as closely as possible, typically five feet off the ground.

Ed started to sweat, and he didn't sweat in the cockpit often. While the Blackhawk's smooth controls responded to Gonzales' movements like a dream, the Little Bird pilots had to work the controls with all their strength.

Jake and the other Razor operatives felt every element, from the freezing desert air to the jerky nature of the flight characteristics. It was a workout to fly it on a normal mission. This was anything but a normal mission, and their muscles felt it.

Seen from above, the line of helicopters resembled a three-car bullet train, speeding just above the desert floor, ready to ram into whatever it found at its destination.

Highway 715, Syria

"Dom, you with me?" Jessie didn't hear Dom's pistol anymore. He feared he was dead. Jessie didn't want to let up his fire at the men behind the trucks; he was hitting them steadily if not killing them. *But how many are there?* he thought.

Suddenly the highway was illuminated with the lights from the two semis they had passed earlier.

The drivers approached the chaos with screeching brakes. Jessie took the distraction as a chance to reposition himself and check on Dominic.

"Talk to me, Dom." Jessie moved him from the front of the bullet-ridden car closer to the back wheel, trailing blood; Dominic was alive, barely. Jessie saw the slide was back on Dominic's pistol.

Dominic spoke, almost a whisper. "I couldn't change the mag."

Jessie let go of his machine gun and changed Dom's magazine, then put it back in his hand.

"Thanks," he whispered.

Rounds hit the car again. Dominic moved his arm like a sloth, aimed at the feet he could see from under the car. With only one working eye, he put a 9mm in the man's knee. When he dropped, he put another in his head. Dominic wasn't dead yet.

The truck drivers were terrified to be in the middle of a firefight, and as soon as they pulled to a stop they opened their doors, fell out, and ran into the safety of the dark desert.

Jessie saw them run for their lives, and his first thought was to somehow get to the cab of the truck and take it. But there was no way he could move Dominic. There were too many men in the way to kill. Jessie stood and resumed shooting at the men spotlighted by the beam of the truck headlights. He got off three rounds before his magazine was spent.

He swore, dropped down, replaced the magazine, and stood up once again. Bullets hit the engine block, the side, the rear. Their cover was disappearing. *This is it. Dom can't move. Last mag, thirty rounds, plus your pistol, and Dom's. This is doable. You need to pick 'em all off, one by one. How many? Ten, maybe? For now. You're a Frogman, you're not getting paid to die. Just kill them.*

With a rifle he could have made short work of the undisciplined men across the way. He wasn't a sniper, but he could knock down bad guys all day long. Unfortunately he was using a weapon designed more for speed and versatility than long range accuracy. In the dark, with no night vision capabilities, bleeding from a dozen of his own wounds, it was a street fight. Jessie dropped one man, tried to ignore the muzzle flashes of their weapons, and pulled the trigger again. He dropped another. Suddenly he felt bullets rip through the broken back window into his waist, pulling him backward.

He struggled to remain standing, thrust himself forward on the car, and propped up his gun. He looked through the ring at the end of the short barrel and was ready to squeeze the trigger again when he heard something that reminded him of a helicopter rotor, and an engine flare up. It was familiar. *Blackhawk?*

The small truck in front of Jessie began shredding, like a log getting cut by a chainsaw. Steel and body parts mixed in a cascade of ghastly fireworks as the Blackhawk pitched to the right, moved into a hover, and let its right door gunner open up with his minigun.

Jessie looked up and turned halfway around; he saw the inky shape moving in the air behind him, and the yellow glow of the minigun's beautiful muzzle flash. Jessie looked back at the carnage in front of him and saw men scrambling away from the vehicle. He felt relief for a moment, then pain. His legs gave way and he slumped forward and hugged the car. He rotated to face the helicopter, and his back slid down the side of the car until he was sitting on the sand.

Jessie looked to his right, saw Dominic lying face down, arm outstretched under the car, still holding the gun. He couldn't tell if he was alive or dead. He tried to call out, but his voice failed. He turned his attention back to the Blackhawk. Its gunner let up. Jessie couldn't see the man's face, but he knew he was looking at him. He struggled to take breaths.

Everything was hazy, slow. Jessie closed his eyes, summoned enough strength to speak, but in a whisper.

"We made it, Dom."

They were the last words he ever spoke.

———

"Marathon, this is Star Two, do you copy? Over." Gonzales had been trying to contact the men on the ground ever since he passed over the border. Now he could see two shapes he assumed must be the Americans on the ground. The copilot raised headquarters, who watched helplessly as they tried to vector the helicopters in to assist Marathon before the clock expired.

"Marathon is not responding but I have visual. Neither is moving. They're in pretty bad shape."

"Copy, we see that, Star Two. Try to avoid hitting the semis if you can."

"Copy that."

"There are two unarmed civilians on the other side of the highway as well."

"Copy that. Star Four, you got 'em?"

"Copy Star Two, I see 'em."

Ed Tanner sized up the situation he was racing into. Dead ahead, he had four small trucks and an SUV on the highway with military-aged men moving all around them, several more dead on the road. To his left were the remains of a small car, shot-up and smoking, with two figures almost underneath it. Hovering to the left of them was Star Two.

Ed saw the Blackhawk door gunner stop firing as his targets scattered in order to hide from the Blackhawk. The armed figures lined up between the semis that were parked side by side. They had no clue Ed was charging straight at their flank.

"Nice of them to line up for us," Jordan said next to him.

"Right."Star Four selected his minigun and let loose a strafe through the trench between the semis, igniting all four vehicles before making a perforation of destruction between the large trucks. As he passed over them, he pulled up, banked to the right, and made a large turn to locate movement on the other side of the highway. He spotted two figures in the infrared, huddled with their foreheads in the sand, hands on the backs of their heads.

The Blackhawk pilot tried one more time. "Marathon, this is Star Two, copy?" No response. "Star Three, insert your team. Star Four, cover us."

"Copy that." Ed was already lining up for a second pass.

"Copy that," Star Three's pilot said. He dropped his Little Bird directly behind the Blackhawk whose door gunner cut down men leaking out from under the semis. His skids touched the sand forty feet away from Marathon's car. As soon as Jake and the three Razor operators hopped off, the Little Bird was airborne again, peeling right to get into the fight.

As the four Americans approached the car, they kept the lifeless shapes in their cross hairs. One was lying down, the other sitting against the tire, staring at them.

The first thing Jake noticed was that they didn't look anything like Americans. Jake saw two dead or dying Middle Eastern men, and was confused. He wondered if they landed on the wrong side of the road.

Jake looked at Jessie. There was no motion, no acknowledgment. His hand was still gripping the handle of a weapon, lifelessly. Razor One crept up to Jessie, gently kicked the weapon out of his hand.

"Check him out," he told Jake, and then turned his attention to the trucks.

The millisecond it took for Jake to look into the man's vacant eyes seemed like an eternity. He was too late. *Are they both gone?* Jake put a hand on his neck; no pulse. He saw the hole in the man's torso, there was nothing he could have done. *Damn.*

Jake turned his attention to Dominic. The coagulating blood pool beneath him was massive. Jake saw something familiar in his mustached face; it reminded him of the man in his nightmares. He paused, but a burst of shots from Razor One's rifle snapped him back. He got up close to Dominic and felt for a pulse. It was almost non-existent. Jake assessed breathing — almost none. He pulled out his flashlight and ran it over Dominic's face. There was a slight blink in the man's good eye. Dominic spoke, but Jake couldn't make it out, so he leaned in to the dying man's ear.

"Don't try to speak. Save your strength. I've got you," Jake said.

Again Dominic tried to speak. "Backpack. Intel."

Jake looked around but didn't see a backpack. "Alright, got it. Save your strength. We'll get it."

Dominic closed his eyes.

"Razor One, you've got five or six under the truck closest to you," the Blackhawk copilot relayed to the assault team on the ground.

"Copy that, Star Two," Razor One said. He looked down at Jake, "Well?"

"This one needs immediate evac. Other guy's KIA."

"Copy." Then into the radio, "Star Two, we're bringing you one KIA, and one alive. Stand by."

"Copy, Razor."

Star Four chimed in. "I count at least seven hiding under the north truck. Engaging."

Ed dropped the Little Bird almost onto the ground and Jordan selected the smaller caliber gun. He was at face level with three men who were trying to hide under the scanty cover the truck provided. The Little Bird gave a short burst, careful to avoid the truck's undercarriage.

———

"We need to move him fast, he's almost gone. Get him on a stretcher," Jake said.

The leader yelled to his men over the helicopter noise.

"Get a stretcher and a body bag."

Jake wanted to move Dominic to the Blackhawk, but knew he was almost bled out; he needed to get fluids into him. Jake stuck him and started the IV, then did a quick test of pulse and breathing. There were so many holes to patch he didn't know if he had enough bandages. He heard the Little Birds buzzing around, shooting intermittently. *Just get in the air, then get to work.* They rolled Dominic onto his back and lifted him onto the stretcher.

"Move him to the bird," Jake said, then went to Jessie. He noticed the backpack strapped to his back. Jake pulled out his knife and cut the straps of the backpack.

Razor One came up and knelt beside Jake. "Here," he said, unfolding a body bag.

They eased Jessie's body into the black bag as gently as possible. Jake took the backpack by the top handle with his right hand and the strap of the body bag in his left, and they hustled to the Blackhawk to join the others onboard.

"This is Star Two, Marathon One and Two on board. Star Three, Star Four. Let's get outta here."

"Copy that," the Little Bird pilots acknowledged.

The Blackhawk lifted up and turned its nose toward the direction they'd come. Star Three covered him from one direction. Star Four continued to circle the semi-trucks, waiting for a clear shot at the men around and under them.

Dawson watched the Little Bird move around the periphery of the screen. He was wavering on whether or not to destroy the trucks, but they couldn't see any clear targets under them. There were two unarmed non-combatants nearby, and taking out the trucks would probably kill them, too. The car was another matter. It undoubtedly contained sensitive CIA intelligence — passport, weapons, laptops.

"Take out the car," Dawson ordered.

The communications officer relayed the order, "Star Four, destroy the car to the west of the semis."

———

Ed Tanner watched the other helicopters get safely away before he circled back in a wide arc. He surveyed the trucks one last time, then took aim of what was left of the small car. Jordan pulled the trigger and released his Hellfire missiles. The car disintegrated in a flash.

"Target destroyed," he said.

"Copy, Star Four, we confirm," the surveillance officer said over the radio.

"Star Two, Star Three, we're done here," Ed said.

"Copy that."

"Well, it's been fun Syria, but I think we'll be going now," Ed said.

"Right," Jordan agreed.

———

When the first helicopter arrived, Khalid was getting ready to bum rush the car that protected the Americans. He was stunned by the sight of the lead truck getting destroyed out of nowhere. The glowing yellow light of the Blackhawk's minigun lit the sky and he didn't fully comprehend it was a helicopter until it began moving toward him, and the men around him began scrambling for their lives. He ran as well.

Some ran between the trucks; others ran into the open and began unloading their AKs into the sky. Khalid crawled under the cab of the large semi truck and hid beside the huge tire. He curled into a fetal position and prayed, fearing every moment his back would be torn open by bullets as everything else around him was. Another helicopter swooped in and shot up the pavement between the trucks. Debris, lead, brass casings, and all variety of carnage washed under the cab of the large truck as he screamed.

But the wave passed. He heard more helicopter noise and dared to open his eyes, but could see little more than grease-covered axels and the large tires. Still, he hid for what seemed like forever. Khalid waited, hoping Allah might spare him.

An accusing voice began to speak. It mocked, like always.

You traitor. You filthy coward. Your brothers lie martyred around you while you cower and weep. Infidels are swarming around the sky of your country, and you hide. You disgust me. You deserve a dog's death.

Khalid was angry. He inched his way forward to look for his rifle on the ground next to him. He moved backward, past the tires, and rolled to face the sky, but he saw nothing.

Where are they? he wondered. He'd missed his moment of greatness, failed to defeat the infidels. Then he heard an explosion. Khalid was filled with rage and joy. *Glory be to the one who's given me chance at redemption.* He smiled and ran around to the front of the truck. There it was, another helicopter. Khalid raised his AK-47, pointed it toward the small round helicopter and squeezed the trigger. The rifle sprayed wildly but Khalid held it firm, screaming as the magazine emptied.

———

Some of the thirty rounds missed the Little Bird entirely. The ones that didn't tore through the small cabin, disturbing metal, glass, and plastic as they ricocheted throughout the cockpit, some of it passing through Jordan's neck. Ed felt the pinging of the rounds and jerked the stick forward to increase speed.

"We're taking fire. We're taking fire," Ed said.

Jordan didn't answer.

On instinct, Jordan put his hand to his neck, distracted by the survival instinct. After several seconds, his brain began to process the competing priorities of keeping himself alive versus flying a helicopter. Avionics training took over and he tried to use his left arm to assist Ed in controlling the machine. But he was also dying.

"Looks alright. We good?" Ed asked Jordan.

Jordan tried to speak but all that came out was gurgle. He clamped his chin to his chest in a daze.

They were shoulder to shoulder in the small cockpit. "Jordan?"

Stealing glances while flying the racing helicopter as it tried to catch up with the other two, Ed saw Jordan holding his neck and sinking forward inch by inch. He realized his copilot was hit, maybe bleeding out.

"Star Three, Star Two, my copilot is hit. Looks pretty bad."

18

Jake

Iraq/Syria Border

Jake's Blackhawk pitched in a new direction every few minutes. Medical monitors screamed but were drowned out by the noise of wind and twin turbo shaft engines at max power. A man covered from head to toe with holes lay on a stretcher beneath him; beams of two small flashlights the only light source as he assessed the injuries with an Army Ranger assisting him.

Jake was finally home.

He didn't relish seeing a man in trauma, but this was his calling, the place he most wanted to be — not because he got a kick out of the action (though he did) but because more than anything else Jake wanted to save lives. His entire focus was on the mustached man under his hands.

He worked fast. All the operators in the Blackhawk had combat first aid training, and the Ranger was a medic in his own right, but for this caliber of veterans, rank mattered little. They all recognized Jake's authority within the eighty-four square feet they shared, and did their best to help or stay out of his way.

Dominic had bullet wounds in the legs, torso, buttock, shoulder and arms. He was bleeding from too many deep lacerations to count. He'd lost over a liter of blood, maybe two, which Jake was trying to replenish while pushing fluids. The Ranger kept tearing open packages of quick-clot combat gauze while trying to locate and plug all of the holes, but the gunshots were not the biggest problem. Dominic was unconscious, heartbeat too slow, breathing too shallow. He crashed for the second time.

Jake shocked his heart and got it pumping again, only to see it slow to almost nothing. There was only so much he could do. How many times could he jump start Dominic's heart before he'd have to call it? Jake was raised to improvise. If plan A didn't work, come up with a new plan. If B failed, try another, and on and on. *Work the problem, there's always a solution.*

Gonzales wanted to fly higher to avoid dangers on the ground but Jake wanted him lower to allow more oxygen.

"Affirmative," Gonzales said, "but it's gonna get wild back there." Jake was willing to take the risk. He was used to the chaos, and the speed mattered as much as the science. *You're not gonna die, brother.*

———

"Jordan, what's up buddy? You hit?"

Ed could tell his copilot was alive. Jordan's hands were moving, trying to assist with flying, but something was certainly not right. He wouldn't speak, wouldn't move his head. He kept his chin down against his chest. Jordan was struggling. Against what, Ed had no idea. Labored breathing kept coming from Jordan's microphone.

"Star Two, he won't reply." Ed got an idea. "Jordan, thumbs up, thumbs down. Can you breathe?"

Jordan raised his left arm slightly and gave thumbs down. He slumped into the side door, still moving his arm but not moving his head.

"Star Two, he can't breathe. We need to get him onto your bird, now."

"Copy, Star Four," Gonzales said. He was already pushing hard to get past hostile territory and get his casualty to the base surgeons as fast as possible. But he knew Jordan — they all did — and he knew Ed. If Ed said something had to happen now, it wasn't a suggestion. Jordan was dying and Star Two was a flying ambulance. He had to get him on board.

"Star Three, I'm gonna put her down. Cover us while we transfer him."

———

Dominic's heart beat again. *But for how long?*

Jake had him on a Lidocaine drip to regulate the heartbeats, but he kept crashing, despite three pints of blood. Jake estimated he must have lost at least thirty percent of his volume, maybe forty. His heart couldn't maintain the pressure and circulation. Dominic's organs were beginning to fail.

One of the flight engineers inched his way to Jake, careful not to step on anything important since there were cords, packages, and tubes all over the place. He leaned in close to Jake and tapped the PJ on the shoulder. "We're gonna land here."

Thank God. Then he realized they couldn't possibly be to Mosul yet.

"Why?" Jake asked, without taking his eyes off Dominic.

"Star Four's copilot is shot. They need you to bring him on board," the man said.

"Copy that," Jake said. *One more to the party.* "How bad?"

"Pretty bad. He's not breathing, we think," the flight engineer said.

Jake swore to himself. *Not breathing. It might be too late already. How long has he been suffocating?* Jake looked out the window and saw one of the Little Birds. It was lighter out, the sun was beginning to rise, still too dark to make out details, but Jake could tell it must be the other bird's crew that was in trouble. The pilot that looked at Jake through the window was expressionless.

The Blackhawk landed faster and softer than Jake thought possible. He rose from his kneepads and stepped over Dominic. "Stay here, and do compressions if we lose him again," he said to the Ranger. "I'll be right back. Make some room."

"Copy that, bro."

Jake pointed to Razor One. "Come with me."

They jumped out of the Blackhawk and saw the Little Bird landing barely far enough away to prevent the two helicopters' blades from hitting. Jake didn't have far to run. He went up to the door but saw Ed giving him a two-finger wave to move around to the other door.

Jake went around and opened Jordan's door, looked at his eyes. They were terrified. Jordan's mouth was open, his chin clamped to his chest. Jake could tell he was alert, breathing even, but…what?

"What's up buddy?"

Jordan motioned with his eyes, tried to speak but nothing but a gurgle came out. Jake tried to ease Jordan out of the copilot's seat. As soon as he put his arm behind him, Jordan lifted his chin and exposed his open neck wound. Blood poured out. His throat was sliced by the bullet and his posture was the only thing pinching the artery. Jordan immediately passed out, stopped breathing and fell out of the seat into Jake.

They lowered Jordan to the ground with Jake pressing hard on his neck. Jake's first instinct was to establish an airway right there on the ground, but then he realized he could see everything around him. Dawn was coming and the helicopters were sitting ducks, even with Star Three's cover. The door of the Blackhawk was mere feet away.

"Let's move him on board. Let's go."

They carried his limp body and hoisted him into the helicopter. Jake got down on his kneepads next to Jordan. He needed to establish an airway, but Jordan's neck was a mess.

He had to decide how to get the air flowing. The gurgling sound when Jordan tried to speak indicated blood was in his airway.

There were three ways to get Jordan breathing again and all involved sliding tubes into the openings in Jordan's head. His neck had suffered severe damage from the flying debris. At least one artery was severed and bleeding through the bandages. There was also the likelihood of spinal damage. Jake peeled the bandage back to see if he could intubate and immediately ruled it out. *Wow. I've never seen that before.*

There was an open hole where his throat should have been, filled with foreign objects Jake couldn't identify. Air and blood — and maybe plastic or glass — were going down it. He saw an air-bubble rise. Jake removed a small plastic tube from its package and slid it into what was left of the opening. Next, he slid a tubular rubber stick known as a bougie into the hole. He slid a larger tracheotomy tube over the bougie which guided it in. When the larger tube was at the proper depth, Jake removed the bougie. He had an airway. Next he needed to get the blood out of Jordan's lungs, but as he reached for the tube he saw the Ranger doing chest compressions on Dominic.

"He keeps crashing," the Ranger said through his own labored breathing.

"Just keep going. Keep his heart pumping. Give me a sec," Jake said.

Jake used suction to clear the new airway and saw Jordan's chest begin to rise and fall. *Good.* He taped an oxygen source to the tube in Jordan's throat. *Now let's see about that artery.* He reached into Jordan's throat again and looked around. *The carotid artery. His brain isn't getting blood flow. He's going to start losing brain functions soon.*

Jordan's carotid artery was almost severed below the bifurcation, the fork-like intersection that joined the three channels of blood flow within his neck: two up toward his head, and one larger channel toward the heart. None of the blood was getting to either of the upper channels that carried blood in and out. It needed to be repaired with immediate surgery. Jake knew how but it was best left to the surgeons. Of course, if they didn't get him on a table soon, it wouldn't matter much.

Jake clamped above and below the hole in the artery, then tried to see what else was in there. He saw a piece of something dark, maybe hard plastic or metal, stuck into the inside of the neck cavity. Jake bandaged it up, careful not to move the object or create more hemorrhaging.

The Blackhawk tilted, and Jake had to hold on to keep his balance. The Ranger stopped compressions; Dominic's heart was beating, barely. His blood pressure was still dangerously low. Jake relaxed a little now that both patients were breathing, it meant he could focus on patching up some of the leaks in Dominic's body, and there were plenty. He felt up and down the older man's frame, rolled him and found exit wounds across his length. He cut loose most of his clothing and covered him with blankets to try to keep him warm. Dominic was almost stable, but then his heart stopped again.

Jake wanted to punch something. He went through a mental checklist. *We shocked him twice. Dosed with Epinephrine, then Lidocaine. There was rhythm, but faint. It comes, then goes. What is the root? He's not getting enough blood. Something else? He looks like he's in his fifties. Middle Eastern. Hypovolemia? Electrolyte imbalance? Maybe a hole in his lung, bullet fragments, a tear. Just keep him alive and let the surgeons figure it out. He's got so many different rhythms. Work the problem, Jake.*

He switched spots with the Ranger, took over chest compressions, and realized it was a matter of whose heart would give up first – Jake's, or his patient's. He looked at the monitors. It came down to whether or not there was still brain function. *How much blood is this heart pumping? Is he already a vegetable?*

Jake continued compressions and stared at the body bag, struggling to keep his focus and balance in the jostling cabin of the Blackhawk. He looked back at his patient and studied the face; it didn't look American. He resembled another, the one Jake saw in his nightmares. He looked at the mustache and thinning hair and saw the face of the man he had aimed at over a year ago when Hondo burst into flames along with people he loved. Jake began to sweat, but not from the chest compressions. *This isn't him. This might be an American, or an ally.* He got angry. He was angry at the loss of life, at war, at being away from Cynthia.

But as fast as the thoughts came, they passed. No, he was not a quitter. He never quit. He wouldn't quit on this man, either.

Jake looked again at the black body bag.

"Hey," he said to Razor One. "Can you reach into my left leg pocket?"

The team leader pulled out the carefully-packed American flag. He didn't need to ask what Jake wanted it for. He unfolded it. As he did, Razor Eight helped him straighten it out. As gently as they could, the Army Rangers laid it over the top of the black body bag.

Jake continued chest compressions. *They've got a chance, anyway.* He looked in Dominic's partially open eye, his face familiar for all the wrong reasons. Jake leaned in and spoke to him, but more to himself.

"Don't give up. You need to fight, brother." Jake continued chest compressions, looked at Jordan's limp body lying next to Dominic. *He needs blood to his brain. This is taking too long.*

"How far out?" Jake asked the pilot over the radio.

The Blackhawk leaped a power line and then flew down again, sending everyone momentarily airborne before slamming to the floor. The pilot answered, "Twenty minutes."

Twenty minutes. In twenty minutes, Jordan might never pick up his kids again. In twenty minutes, he may never walk, or speak, certainly never fly. Jake made a decision.

"Take over," he told the Ranger.

They switched and Jake pulled the bandages away from Jordan's neck, exposing the clamps on the artery.

That others may live. He had always believed the Pararescue motto referred to survival, but it really meant more than that; Aiden was living proof. He used to be here, patching guys up to keep them alive. But he couldn't do this anymore, so he changed the narrative. He changed his definition of what it means to live. Living means more than surviving, it means coming home and being able to really love their families; to hold them, be intimate or cry alongside them when their minds or hearts are broken. Aiden had helped Jake live again. He wanted that for this pilot, as well.

In a surgery one would methodically peel back layers of tissue protecting the artery, but Jordan's was already exposed. Jake braced himself to steady his arms as he used tweezers to hold and then trim edges of the artery. The Rangers craned their necks to watch over Jake's shoulder.

He used three narrow tubes in a Y-shape to create an arterial intersection. He gently slid one end into the large lower part of the artery, then did the same with the small upper interior and exterior channels. When they were in far enough, Jake tightened the connections with a suture around each tube, and then held his breath as he removed the clamps. The blood flowed through the bypass. Jake watched it for half a minute. Satisfied it wasn't causing more harm than good, he covered the neck wound and took Jordan's vitals. He prayed it might make a difference, and hoped the surgeons wouldn't tell him he screwed something up.

Jake looked up at the Ranger still doing uninterrupted compressions on Dominic. He was thoroughly engrossed with what he'd just witnessed.

"Want me to take a turn?" Jake asked.

"No way, bro. I got this. You just keep doing what you're doing. Nice work."

Jake went back to Jordan. *I hope so.*

Flying behind them, Ed Turner also hoped and prayed as he flew the Little Bird. He wasn't crying, but he knew he might be later, when he'd have to tell Jordan's wife and two boys what happened to their dad.

———

Twenty minutes later the Blackhawk landed and Jake and the Ranger medic were met on the tarmac by the base hospital staff. As they wheeled Dominic and Jordan into the hospital, Jake gave a brief summation of all he'd done to the patients. The hospital workers simply took over without any commentary or questions, and wheeled the patients away.

In the blink of an eye, Jake was a bystander, unneeded, and in the way with all of his bulky gear. He and the Ranger turned and exited the same way they'd come. When he was back outside he was met by Razor One.

"Nice job. They gonna make it, you think?" he asked.

"I hope so."

The Ranger captain put his arm around the PJ. "I'm glad you're here. Get some grub and some sleep. Stand down for the rest of the day, call home. Let 'em know you're alive. You have anybody you need to check in with?"

Jake thought for a moment. "Yeah, actually, I do. A couple of people."

———

The next day Jake sat by himself in the mess hall, finishing a pile of food, while scribbling on a sticky note. A thin man with graying hair approached him.

"Do you mind if I sit?" the Army surgeon said.

"Sure," Jake said scooping the sticky notes into a pile and putting them in a zipper baggie.

"I don't mean to intrude."

"Not at all. Just notes to send to my wife. I find it easier to jot short notes when I can versus writing a long letter."

"It's a great idea. You're the PJ who brought in the pair last night, right?"

"Yeah. I'm Jake," he said extending his hand.

"Scott," the doctor said, shaking it.

He poured some milk into a bowl of oatmeal and raisins. "You saved them both. I don't know if you knew that or not. You did a great job…although you best never perform a CEA in the field again. Lucky for you, it was perfect."

Jake's heart beat a little faster, like a kid afraid of the punishment his teacher was about to dish out. He knew he shouldn't have performed the complicated carotid endarterectomy, but he knew he did it right. "Uh, sorry. I just…"

Scott smirked, "Save it. But I have to know, where did you train?"

"All over, really. I learned a bunch riding with EMTs in Boston. Saw some crazy stuff there."

"Oh yeah? Before I got called up I was an ER doc at BMC."

Jake smiled and shook his head. Boston Medical Center was one of the busiest emergency rooms in the country. He leaned back in his chair. "Then I don't have to tell you. You've got some stories to tell me, I'll bet. That place is unreal."

Scott smiled and stirred his oatmeal. "Kinda like here but with better restaurants."

"And more cooperative patients," Jake said.

Scott laughed. "Yeah, this one time we had two guys come in at once. Cut each other up in a knife fight or something, pretty similar to the neck wound you had yesterday."

They traded stories for the next hour – two generations of men gleaning wisdom from each other, proud of their work, but both knowing sometime soon the outcome would be different. Their work never stopped for long and they certainly couldn't save everyone. But they would try.

PART IV

19

Stars

Langley, VA 2008

CIA Director Green looked at his watch. It was time. He closed the dossier and placed it atop the stack on his desk.

He stole a brief glance at the events schedule for the upcoming ceremony. There was a lot to prepare for; the President would be here again. There would be family members in attendance to honor, a speech of his own to practice, and more. There was also a war to run, and a country needing to know what his agency was doing to win it. There were a hundred little things to attend to that he couldn't leave to a subordinate — wouldn't leave to a subordinate. He didn't have time, but he would make time.

They deserve it.

Green stretched his back and walked out of his office to the elevator, pushing the button for the lobby. When the doors opened again, he stepped out and saw several colleagues in business attire standing around. Nobody paid attention to the director, one of the most powerful men in the world. They were all watching someone else.

Nobody spoke. There was no chitchat, nobody stealing the ear of an agency higher up, no posturing or pandering.

Green also found a place to watch. A number of CIA employees of all levels, alongside service workers and maintenance men, were stopped in the course of their daily duties, all watching. Nobody would tell them to hurry back to work. Nobody would begrudge the lost productivity. What they were watching used to be rare, but had become common in the last several years.

The closest onlookers were a respectful distance behind the man with the pneumatic air hammer and chisel, who seemed oblivious to the crowd as he went about his work along the wall of white marble, gleaming in its sterile white surroundings. He had already completed the detailed measurements. Each of the four stars he was about to carve into the memorial wall in the lobby of the Central Intelligence Agency headquarters was mapped out for him, long before he was asked to perform the work. Director Green himself made the final decision as to what spot on the marble wall the craftsman would carve on. It was not a decision made lightly.

The wall was magnificent in its simplicity, just an inscription at the top that read, *In Honor of Those Members of the Central Intelligence Agency Who Gave Their Lives in the Service of Their Country.*

For many years, there had been just three rows of black stars below the inscription. Now there were five rows, soon to be six. In a bullet-proof display case below the wall of stars sat an opened book listing most of the names represented by the stars, but not all. Over thirty of the stars commemorated anonymous individuals, whose sacrifice remained secret. Few people knew who they were.

Included in this latter group was one of the four being carved today.

Director Green was one of the few who knew the recipient. Not personally, not by reputation; the man was just a name, his story just a story — one that the director could not officially confirm, even to the star's family. *Maybe someday, I hope.*

Green was humbled as he watched the dust of the marble chip away. His eyes began to well up, and he was strong enough not to try to hide it.

When he began his tenure, there were far fewer stars on this wall. The Cold War claimed less than fifty; the War on Terror more than twice that in a fifth of the time. Green was present when the mason carved all of them; he owned the losses. Green knew all of their stories and personally contacted the families whenever able.

Jeremiah Tolloson, "Jessie" to his former SEAL fraternity, his ex-wife, and fifteen-year-old daughter, was listed in the CIA Memorial Honor Book with a simple gold star under the 2008 heading.

Eventually Green would meet select members of his family in a private meeting, read an official commemoration he didn't write, vague on details, and hand them their own carved marble star while reminding them of the extreme need for secrecy, lest other families receive similar mementos.

Over the course of its history, some CIA families were told fairy tales about their loved ones. Green changed all that. He didn't always know the whole story, but he flat out refused to tell a family member a falsehood. They would receive the truth or nothing, and Green ensured it fell to him to explain why. He didn't know if he would have to look Jessie's daughter in the eye or not, or his father or mother. When that day came, Green would ask God's guidance for how to ease their pain, how to convey the fact that their son, or her father, had literally bled to death to save a man he hardly knew, in a place Green couldn't name, in a scenario he couldn't describe.

But he would be sure to tell them that without Jessie's tenacity, training, and sacrifice, the four stars being etched on the wall this year would have been five.

Syracuse, NY

The phone rang. Constance looked at her clock, *11:45pm.* She and her husband shared a look on the sofa. *Who would be calling at this hour?* She walked to the counter and picked up the handset.

"Hello?"

"Hi, is this Connie?"

"Yes. Dad? Is that you?" she said.

"Hi, sweetie."

"Dad…wow, it's been a while."

"I know, I'm sorry. You know how it is."

"Yeah," she said as she sat on the sofa next to her husband, who leaned in so they could both hear. "Are you home? Or are you working?" she asked.

"I'm in Germany. But I'll be coming home, in a month maybe, they think."

"What?" She paused. "Dad, are you alright?"

There was a long pause on Dominic's side of the phone.

"No, but I will be. At least that's what they're telling me. I'm gonna be on the sidelines for a while though, and I'm coming home. It'd be nice to see you all."

"Yeah, of course. I don't suppose you're able to tell me what happened?" She knew the answer. For her entire thirty-one years, Connie's father had been absent for months, years at a time. He was always full of smiles and souvenirs on return, but never once was he able to tell her where he'd been, or where or when he was leaving next.

"I got into a scrap. Got beat up a little. Not much more to say."

"But you're okay?" Her husband had his arm around her now.

"Yes."

"Well, good. Maybe now you'll listen about retiring."

Dominic chuckled, then winced from the pain. "Yeah, maybe this time you might get somewhere." There was an awkward pause before he continued. "How are the kids? Jamie?"

"We're all good. Jamie's still teaching. Kids are all fine, they're in bed."

"Sorry, I forgot about the time."

"No, I'm glad you called."

"Going to be having any more soon?"

"Maybe?" she laughed. "But I think we'll just sit on four for now. Heck, you've never even met Lina yet."

"Well, hopefully I'll be in Maryland soon, so maybe in a few I can come up?" Connie's husband gave her a thumbs up.

"Anytime, Dad."

"Thanks." Another pause. "So, how's your Mama doing?"

"I guess she's fine. Moved up to the Bay Area, I think. We don't really talk."

"Well, I understand that."

"Oh, I'm sure you do. Dad…are you sure you're alright?"

Dominic looked at the tubes coming from his body, the sterile walls of the hospital room, the charts on the door. He reflected on Jessie, on dozens of years of service, on the increasing number of friends and acquaintances lost in the last seven.

"Well, sweetie, it's like I said. No, but I will be."

20

Their Places

Tucson, Arizona

The huge C-17 Globemaster finally pulled to a stop. Inside, men and women were lined up in rows, anxious to descend the ramp and greet the throngs of sign-wavers on the tarmac. They were finally home. Most of them.

Arizona was not home to the airman stepping off the plane. Nobody on the tarmac waited for him, no girlfriend, no parents. The few friends he had in town would probably be surprised to know he was back, and his best friends in the world were right beside him, getting ready to absorb their wives and kids for the foreseeable future. He was excited for them. The officers and older guys mostly had families with kids of all ages. The younger ones had enthusiastic girlfriends who lost all composure at times like this. Some had new babies they'd only ever seen over Skype or email. Some had wives with bulging baby bumps after the six-month deployment.

It would be a day of reunion and tears. For him, it was merely a day nobody was likely to take a shot at you, in a place where the air didn't smell like garbage.

The line of men snaked off the ramp into the sun. As a wave of applause preceded the excited cries of children, he smiled. Families tried to obey the security perimeter but very soon the human tide burst from its invisible container and washed over the men and women in uniform. Fathers stooped low with arms opened wide to greet their kids. Husbands and boyfriends embraced their camouflage-clad beauties, and tried, and failed, not to cry themselves. Fathers patted their sons on the back and then gave them hugs tighter than either expected.

He walked through the crowd; his smile fading with every step. He wasn't feeling sorry for himself. Rather, he felt out of place, awkward, an intruder into something sacred. He wanted out of there, fast. He quickened his pace and hoped he could escape without anyone noticing. He didn't have a destination — probably just back to his sparsely-decorated apartment and his video game console, maybe picking up some pizza and a six-pack of beer on the way. He prayed none of the TV camera crews or photographers would approach him. He tried not to look anyone in the eye, but with so many people, it was hard not to.

His eye was naturally drawn to a young girl sitting on her dad's shoulders. Her smile was contagious. His eyes followed her dangling legs down toward what was probably her sister hanging onto the man's back. He recognized Master Sergeant Hector Galindo. He tried to look away but couldn't help noticing that Sergeant Galindo's wife was obviously pregnant, holding his hand as they spoke to someone, smiling and laughing. The man they spoke to was obviously civilian in his shorts and...prosthetic leg.

Maybe he's a veteran. The airman wondered too long, because as soon as the question entered his mind the man turned and looked him in the eye, almost as if he'd heard the thought.

He diverted his eyes and walked on, but his peripheral vision caught a glimpse of the man hugging the Master Sergeant, and then walking in his direction. He tried not to notice, but in a few seconds the man was ahead of him and slowly moving closer, obviously intending to converse. He turned to face him, unsure what to make of the stranger who didn't appear to be a reporter or a photographer, but who was holding a few cards in his hand.

"Welcome back, my name is Aiden." He extended his hand in a professional manner.

"I'm Phillip," he said, shaking hands.

"I'm sorry to bother you, but I wanted to invite you to a thing we've got this afternoon. I'm a veteran. Me and couple of guys are having a low-key barbecue, just a few single guys without families. Here," Aiden handed the card with a map on one side and text and a phone number on the other.

Aiden saw the man studying the card and continued. "Free grub, ribs and steak and such. You don't need to bring anything unless you want to. Come whenever and stay as long as you'd like. No agenda."

"Yeah, alright. Maybe. Thanks," he said, with all the intention of throwing the card away as soon as he was out of sight. He started to walk off.

"Cool. It was nice to meet you, bro. That number on the card is mine. I want to give you permission to call it anytime, for anything. Coming home can be crazy. Sometimes things just seem…off. Ya know? If so, give me a call, no joke," Aiden said, then smiled and walked away.

He stood stunned. He watched the man walk toward the crowd as he paused and hugged another guy, obviously familiar with many in the unit.

The airman hunched his pack tighter and looked again at the card, flipped it over and looked at the map. It was a private residence in a really nice part of town. As the airman walked into the building he thought about his apartment, his meager paycheck, his year-old video games. He walked past a garbage can, and put the note in his pocket.

———

Fayetteville, North Carolina

There was screaming, blood-curdling screaming. The sounds were relentless. Jake sat up in his bed sweating, again

Every night he woke up to the screaming. Every night blended in together. He could hardly rest, hardly function. He was at the end of himself; he didn't know what to do.

Cynthia sat up next to him as she always did.

"It's okay, babe. Go back to sleep," he said.

"Are you sure? You okay?" she asked, but even as the words slid out she was already starting to lie back down.

"Yeah. Good to go," Jake said to the already snoring beauty beside him. But it was another lie. He was lost, scared, and worried about screwing up again. He needed her, more than he ever realized. Often Cynthia would get up with him, nurturing, caring, giving up everything, even sleep to help Jake through any struggle. But she needed rest and they both knew it. This time Jake was on his own.

He put his feet on the floor and pulled on his shorts. The screaming still reverberated in his ears. He got up and stumbled in the dark bedroom, kicked his foot into the doorframe, swore under his breath.

He walked down the dark hallway, hoping against hope the screams would stop. For a moment it seemed they might. But no, there they were again, tormenting more than just him.

Jake walked past the kitchen, saw the bottles strewn across the counter, in the sink. The place was a mess. He didn't care. He needed to stop the screams.

He got to the end of the hallway. With trepidation he put his hand on the doorknob, took a deep breath, and opened it. The screaming was at a fever pitch. *Man up, Jake.* He held his head high, took a bold step into the spare room and walked up to the baby's crib.

"Come on, buddy. You're gonna make me look bad for Mama."

He reached in and scooped the wailing two-month-old into his arms. The baby tilted his head back and trembled while waves of unmet needs rang in Jake's ear. Surely everyone on Earth and in Heaven was listening to the evidence of Jake's ineptitude.

Good God, I've delivered babies, but how on earth do you make one quiet? Milk. He had none. *Cynthia, that showoff.* But he also smelled something and knew what he had to do.

"Come on now. We can get through this together," he said to his son. "Your mom just needs a little rest, okay? I'll buy you a four-wheeler on your sixth birthday if you please just quiet down." But he didn't.

Jake fumbled through the diaper change in the twilight and put the baby's clothes back on, getting the snaps all buttoned in the wrong order. He didn't care. As soon as he picked up the warm little body, his cries diminished to a whimper. Jake gently bounced him; his cries were more evenly spaced now, indicating he might tolerate the feeding delay, but was reserving judgment on the guy with the big green footprint tattoo.

Jake got to the kitchen and leaned forward while holding the baby upright between his chest and left arm, opening the refrigerator door with his right. He found the bottle of milk Cynthia had left for such a time as this. He kept bouncing the baby while he warmed hot water for heating the breast milk. *I'm getting the hang of this.*

"We got this, right, buddy? No worries."

Jake took a swig from the plastic nipple to test the heat and made a face in the dark. It didn't taste bad, but it was weird.

"Not my cup of tea, bro. It's all yours." He offered it to the little man, who began sucking with the first and most natural of all passions, and was finally content.

Praise God.

Jake took a slow walk down the hall to the living room. He paused every few minutes to admire the warm little human cradled against muscles that seemed useless and in the way tonight. His neck began to stiffen and he looked to lie down somewhere. The clock on the wall read 06:45. The bottle was mostly empty and started slipping out of the baby's gaping mouth.

Jake took the bottle and set it on the coffee table, turned the baby around so they were chest to chest and carefully flopped down on the sofa. He looked out the window, at the wall, at the clock and finally at the remote on the table. He reached for it, trying not to wake the baby lying across him. After three tries he reached it and turned on the TV. The volume was too loud and Jake frantically hit the low volume button, hoping not to wake anyone.

He clicked around, ignored all the news channels and settled on a football pregame show. Jake half-watched through slit eyelids. Every few minutes he looked down at the baby on top of him. The boy's breath grew deeper. If he were careful, he figured he could put him back down in his crib, and go back to bed himself.

But he didn't, because he didn't really want to. Jake wanted to soak it in while he had the chance, for a little while anyway.

He knew he'd be deploying soon enough, maybe overseas, maybe for training. He would brave sandstorms and bullets and IEDs or worse, and lose patients and drape American flags over their body bags. All of it was inevitable, Jake knew, because war is inevitable. But today it was someone else's war; someone else would be the hero.

Cynthia walked out to the living room wrapped in her robe, saw her men together in the first beams of morning. She slid in next to Jake, buried her head on Jake's chest, feeling her baby's breath, and hearing Jake's heartbeat.

She would soak in as much as possible while she had the chance, knowing full well there was delicate work for fierce men elsewhere, and guys like her husband were needed.

———

Tel Aviv, Israel

"This should be interesting." The American technician examined the damaged laptop through the sealed plastic container.

"Wow, got a few bullet holes," his Israeli colleague said.

"Sure looks like it," he agreed, opening the package.

Glass and glass dust fell out as he removed the computer from the sleeve. They shared a perplexed look and shook their heads.

The front and back were scratched violently, and two holes revealed that high-caliber bullets had passed through it. Neither technician was shocked; retrieving data from damaged computers and hard drives was their specialty. If it were easy, anybody could do it, and this machine would have been mined for data back in Baghdad.

But there must have been something incredibly valuable on this hard drive. The armed men who brought it in, standing right outside the lab, were evidence of that.

The Israeli turned it over, slowly lifted the screen as the hinges made a crunching sound. He looked at his counterpart. "You guys seen many of these?"

"A few. You?"

"Sure, but they're not usually worth the effort."

"I hear ya. Screen is gone, motherboard is obviously shot, literally."

They closed it and turned it over, began removing screws from the underside. When the components were free they separated the keyboard from the plastic casing and began removing more screws from the interior, freeing components as they went and unplugging them from the motherboard until they got to the hard drive.

"Bullet nicked the hard drive," said the Israeli.

"Not too bad, though. Let's see inside." They opened the hard drive casing to reveal the disk and circuits.

"Went through the PCB. Data should be good," the American said, with obvious relief.

"Yep. Let me find a matching board." The Israeli went to a shelf of plastic bins full of all varieties of parts and components, some new, some recycled. He searched until he found a hard drive that matched the damaged laptop's model.

The disk was unharmed. They tested the transient-voltage-suppression-diode with a multimeter and found it was damaged, so they decided to just rebuild the hard drive from scratch. Unless the data was overwritten, it was still there; it was only a matter of restoring the circuitry and providing a power source to read it.

Two hours passed while they tested the hard drive. Eventually they had the disk in a new drive, confident it would operate. The Israeli attached the rebuilt hard drive to a desktop computer and accessed it via the operating system.

"Alright, let's see what we have here," he said.

Neither of them were intelligence analysts; they were computer technicians for their respective governments, and they worked together from time to time on especially sensitive cases. They both spoke and read Arabic and were experienced enough to know when a hard drive recovered from a terrorist had sufficient information to warrant a high priority analysis.

As the Israeli clicked his mouse and opened Saeed Al-Maquatti's personal files, the men's eyes widened. The American took notes on a pad and paper. More and more files were opened: spreadsheets, maps, sound files, videos, pornography, and dozens of bank account numbers.

After another hour the Israeli sat back and looked at his colleague, then picked up his phone.

The American went to the door of the lab and knocked to alert the security detail on the other side. The security guard nodded through the window, then called someone on his radio.

Soon the world's two most powerful intelligence services were examining and sharing multiple leads with agencies in six western countries, pulling on threads of the terrorist tapestry and forming new counterintelligence plans based on the information gleaned from a broken laptop, found in a blood-stained backpack cut from the shoulders of a man with no name, from nowhere.

21

The Stars and Their Places

Northern Iraq

Ed Tanner went through his pre-fight routine for the night's mission. As he went about his calculations he noticed a beam of red light illuminate his hand, and allowed himself a momentary distraction to look out the window, admiring the setting sun. For many years he had gone about the business of war and paid little mind to things like sunsets, or waterfalls, or the wavy ocean currents he flew his machines of destruction over. Age had taught him the value of pausing to appreciate them. He didn't always get the chances a civilian might, but he knew he was blessed — in a way — for the opportunity to behold beauty in places that others wrote off as hellholes.

Ed watched the setting sun, looked over to Jordan preparing for their first mission together in over a year. He was about to mention the sunset, but stopped when he caught sight of the massive scar across Jordan's neck, peeking above his collar. It held Ed's gaze, though he tried not to stare.

Jordan felt the stare and looked at Ed. "What?" he asked.

"Nothing. We good?" Ed asked.

Jordan knew Ed was referring to the mission, but also much more.

"We own the night," Jordan said.

"Damn right, we do," Ed said.

Ed turned back to the sunset. *Good boy.*

213

Tucson, Arizona

Stacy McCoy sat in her prettiest dress, hating every minute of it. She didn't have anything against dresses; in fact, she liked the one she was wearing, but tonight she *had* to wear it, and that made all the difference. She kicked and swung her legs underneath her chair and prayed that soon it would all be over.

She looked to the right and left, where a half-dozen fellow piano recital victims waited to take their turn in the spotlight. Stacy already had played once; that was the easy number. The next one was more complex, and she was going to be accompanied by her piano teacher. She looked around and saw her mom and two of her brothers; Evan gave her a thumbs up. Her other brother had recently endured his own execution and was free to sit back with victorious hands behind his head, three seats down.

Stacy, her teacher had informed her at the last minute, was the final performer of the night. It was so unfair. She would have to endure the whole thing. To make matters worse, her uncle Aiden was a no-show. It devastated her. Aiden was always there, for everything, and she didn't fully appreciate it until today. Her dad, Josiah McCoy, had deployed with his A-10 squadron almost a year ago. Aiden was not Dad, but she needed him all the same. He had said would be here; he had lied.

Stacy kept an eye on the door the entire recital, every minute hoping Aiden would walk in so she could forgive him. Now there were only two performers left. She looked at the floor, trying hard not to cry.

Abigail was also watching the door, almost willing Aiden to show up. She was surprised when he wasn't there on time, sad when he missed Stacy's first number, annoyed when he missed his nephew's.

It was probably unfair to Aiden, she acknowledged. He gave so much of his time to being there in his brother's place. Part of her wanted Aiden to be free to do bachelor things and unshackle himself from the self-appointed obligations of a father of four. But they needed him. As unfair as it may have been to Aiden, his nephews and niece needed him. Abigail would have been fine with him missing the recital if he had said he couldn't make it, but he had promised Stacy he would be there.

He better be dead or I'm going to kill him.

Abigail repented almost immediately, ashamed of the thought. She prayed silently for Aiden's safety. She looked at the clock, and began planning exactly how and when she would wring her brother-in-law's neck.

Stacy watched the second-to-last performer walk toward the front of the room. She was next; she was defeated. Aiden wasn't coming. She turned and slumped in her chair and considered not playing at all. She was already almost in tears.

With her back to the door, Stacy didn't see Aiden sneak in, but Abigail did. He was smiling. Abigail was incredulous.

How dare he smile!

Aiden saw the death look in her eyes; he knew that look well. But then he went a step too far. He winked at her.

Oh, he's dead. Abigail fumed as she turned away from her smirking little brother-in-law, who always seemed to win, whom everyone loved. Aiden, who simultaneously carried the distinction of being her greatest childhood enemy, and her current best friend — was winking at her. *The audacity.*

But Abigail was not the only one watching the door for

Aiden. Janine, the McCoy's piano teacher, was anxious for his arrival. The fake smile on her face blossomed into a real one. She grinned ear to ear as Aiden made a point of gesturing to her with his eyebrows and smiled.

They were each more excited than either had been in a long time. Both needed a win, a distraction from the stress of the long year. Tonight would be the culmination of their radical conspiracy, the impossible plan Aiden had proposed to her weeks ago.

Janine led the applause for her student. When it died down, she moved to the center of the stage.

"Thank you all for coming out tonight and lending your support to our students. We have one performance left before our recital concludes. For this number Stacy McCoy will be performing, and…" the teacher's voice cracked. She paused to regain composure. "Stacy McCoy will be performing, and I was going to accompany her. However, tonight she will be accompanied by her father, Colonel Josiah McCoy."

The teacher held out her arm with outstretched palm toward the back of the room. Gasps went up all around the room as people shifted across their chairs to look behind them. Abigail dropped her camera and put her hand on her mouth as tears began to stream down her cheeks, starting a chain reaction of similar responses.

Josiah stood in full dress uniform. He put his hat under his arm and walked formally to Stacy, who was shaking and crying. Before he got there, she jumped over the boy sitting next to her and leaped onto her father, causing everyone not already crying to lose it. A second later both of Josiah's older sons were also clinging to him. Abigail stood on wobbly legs and walked up to the cluster of hugging bodies, her hand still over her mouth, holding her toddler's hand with the other.

Josiah saw her and tried to put Stacy down, but she was latched to him as someone drowning clings to anything that floats. Abigail worked her way into the embrace. As soon as she felt his hand on her shoulder, she buried her head in his chest and sobbed. After what felt like an eternity she looked up at him and they kissed. Then she smacked his chest.

"You couldn't give me a little warning?" She was smiling, laughing, and crying all at the same time. "Big jerk. The house is a disaster." She wiped mascara from her eye. "There's laundry all over the sofa."

"Good. I've been wanting to see your underwear for months," Josiah said.

She smacked him again on the chest. "Incorrigible. God, I love you." She laughed and kissed him again.

Aiden watched it unfold in silence. Eventually the crowd began to disperse, Stacy was spared from performing, the piano teacher was congratulated for her part in the conspiracy, and the McCoy family left for two weeks of nothing, except bliss.

———

"So, if I'm hearing ya, son, you've already made up your mind."

Josiah looked across the flames of his grandpa's backyard fire pit, then down at the toddler sitting in his lap, eating a marshmallow.

"We're still weighing the options. It's not like I don't love blowing stuff up, it's just not so much fun turning slow circles over the same grids, and being away from all this…for years…and all these young pups…I just think maybe it's time to hand it over. I don't want to quit on 'em, though."

"It ain't quitting. Look at your brother; did he quit?" he asked, looking at Aiden. "No, he didn't. The circumstances changed and he adapted to them. There is no shame in that, for him or for you, and if moving over to the Air Guard or whichever assignment lets you to best meet the needs of this season, be it your family, your country, or yourself —" he leaned in and looked Josiah in the eye, "— and Josey, it's okay to consider yourself once in a while…then you need to stop beating around the bush, and do it."

The old man sat back, took a sip from his steel coffee mug and looked away. "You can't save everybody, believe me. Sometimes you just need to walk away."

Josiah and Aiden looked at each other. Their grandpa was not usually this talkative and his advice hung in the air for some time. Finally Josiah spoke.

"Part of me just wants to get out altogether. With all these rules of engagement, and what's probably coming down the pike, it's a heck of a lot more fun flying Piper Cubs for hunting trips."

"You'll figure it out, just don't sit around wasting time. You, either," he said, glancing at Aiden.

Aiden and Josiah shared another look.

"Actually, I'm kinda leaning on moving back home," he said.

"'Bout time. Stop hanging around your old girlfriend," Grandpa McCoy said.

"What?" Aiden asked.

Josiah laughed, "What do you mean, 'What?' You know."

Aiden did know. Proximity to his former unit kept him in close contact with people he loved, but it was also painful to be around them, longing for the past. His father once told him, *The best cure for getting over an old girlfriend is a new one*, and Aiden's first and only true love was the PJs.

"Are you happy?" Grandpa McCoy asked.

"Sometimes. Overall, no, I guess. I love being around the kids, and helping guys get back on track is what I'm most passionate about. It's hard to articulate, but it just feels like it's time to move on. This place doesn't feel like it fits anymore. It did for a time, but not now."

"It's just another season, Aiden. They change, you know." He took a sip from his mug, then sighed. "When your grandma died, I had a hard time understanding it myself. I kept sitting around trying to relive that season with memories or pictures and all, but eventually I had to come to the realization that the season had changed and it was time to get to work."

He took another drink, looked up at the stars. "You know how when the snow melts, there's all sorts of garbage to pick up and grass to rake? But if you don't clean it up, you stifle the new growth, right? It's the same with seasons of life. People spend years training up to do something, shine at it for a while, but then the season changes and they need to move on."

They listened to the fire crackling, then he continued. "For some of them the light goes out, and they pine away lamenting the past, regretting or trying to regain it. It was like that for me. My light went dim, almost went out. But other people take it as a new challenge. An adventure, maybe, for some, but it's probably terrifying for most. Uncertainty is scary."

The old man sat, looking at the fire; Aiden and Josiah sat, thinking about his words. Josiah's son squirmed in his lap, asleep, and the boy's sticky fingers fell loose onto his flannel shirt. Josiah and Aiden smiled at the youngest McCoy.

"I agree," Josiah said, "but I'm not afraid of uncertainty. If I were, I never would have lasted in this job. What I fear is the other thing you said, about going dim. I don't want that. I don't want to see that in you, either," he said to Aiden. "I don't think you're the type to stay put for long. You never were. And you shine wherever you go."

Abigail came up behind Josiah and wrapped her arms around his shoulders, put her cheek against his, and admired the toddler in his lap.

"Aww, he fell asleep," she said, smiling. She scooped the boy off him and handed him over to Aiden, then went back to Josiah and got comfortable in his lap, neither of them concerned about the weight limits of the creaking camp chair. Abigail kissed Josiah.

"It's getting late. We should probably head home soon?"

Josiah and Aiden shared a look.
"I think she's right," Josiah said.
"Yeah. She usually is," Aiden agreed.

a preview:

BOOK III

PEGASUS

WONDERLAND

Balad, Iraq
Six months earlier

Porter walked through the plywood maze toward the planning room. He heard booming voices and teasing laughter. The room was full of often-rowdy men in various stages of dress, some in uniform, some in hoodies and flip flops; most had beards. He entered and walked past several men as the laughter died down, and those who were sitting sat up straight. In the rear, a couple of uniformed men held an "at-ease" attention in the corner, looking anything but.

A few nodded. "Skipper," they said, as he walked past.

Porter looked over the crowd of smelly, dangerous men and settled in at the front. A large projection screen was to his left. In front of him was a relief map on a table with a layout of a long streets and several cardboard model buildings. Porter noticed three of the highest-ranking officers in the city slide into the room and stand along the back wall; they were not smiling.

His gaze fell on Tim Miller, standing in his flight suit next to three other pilots. His arms were folded. Porter made eye contact, gave a respectful nod. Tim just stared.

Porter took in the rest of the crowd and began his briefing. "Alright ladies, shut up and listen up. There's gonna be a lot of people watching this one, so dial in. We're moving on this fast and there are a bunch of moving parts, so speak up if you see something. We're calling this op, Wonderland."

The Stars And Their Places is the second book in a four part series that began with *Beyond the Golden Hour* and will continue in *Pegasus*.

ACKNOWLEDGMENTS

The generosity of strangers is often taken for granted. Over the course of this project, I sought advice and assistance from experts in their respective fields many times. So many individuals were exceedingly generous with their time, and the book you're holding wouldn't exist without their help.

To firefighter/EMTs D.J. and Robin, for the spirited roundtable discussions about life-threatening injuries debated over chips and salsa, while my squeamish wife tried not to hear.

To Mike, for bringing a physician's insight to my layman's attempt at explaining medical procedures, and for introducing me to cool terms I'd never heard of, like "bougie." And for bringing coffee.

To David, for praying with me about this project over a year ago and for the thoughtful, timely replies to all of my requests. I am honored to have met you and your beautiful family.

To Clifford, for providing monthly creative writing opportunities, and for the link to the special operations community.

To Brendan, for all of the encouraging emails, fact-checking, and suggestions from an insider's perspective that brought new details and gave me personal understanding into the warrior mind. I truly appreciate your transparency.

To the veterans and their wives who shared their stories and provided feedback and endorsements. I cannot thank you enough.

To Michael, for the beautiful framed photograph in our study taken by a veteran while on duty in Afghanistan, which I look at often, remembering their service.

To Mattie, for patiently guiding me through the labyrinth of Photoshop, and for never shying away from an artistic challenge.

To all of my subscribers and faithful readers who gave time and much-needed morale boosts along the way – Larry and Sharon, Cindy, Chris, Melanie, Keenen, Cody, Paul, Luke, Josh and many more – thank you.

And, of course, my wife Shannon, who once again braved the gore of fictional combat to edit this book in order to deliver a superior read. Moments ago she told me, "It's time for you to get to work."

Indeed.

A FINAL NOTE

This is a work of fiction, but the following resources were influential in grounding the story in reality. I recommend them for anyone interested in the real stories upon which this one is based.

books

The U.S. Army in Iraq: Volume 2, Surge and Withdrawal 2007-2011. U.S. Army Strategic Studies Institute and U.S. Army War College Press, 2019.

Fields of Combat: Understanding PTSD in Veterans of Iraq and Afghanistan by Erin P. Finley, 2008.

War Surgery in Afghanistan and Iraq: A Series of Cases, 2003-2007 by Shawn Christian Nessen, Dave Edmond Lounsbury, and Stephen P. Hetz, 2008.

Relentless Strike: The Secret History of Joint Special Operations Command by Sean Naylor, 2015.

The Night Stalkers: Top Secret Missions of the U.S. Army's Special Operations Aviation Regiment by Michael J. Durant and Steven Hartov, 2008.

None Braver: U.S. Air Force Pararescuemen in the Afghanistan War by Michael Hirsh, 2003

The Last Punisher: A SEAL Team Three Sniper's True Account of the Battle of Ramadi, by Kevin Lacz, Ethan E. Rocke, and Lindsey Lacz, 2016.

The Book of Honor: Covert Lives and Classified Deaths at the CIA by Ted Gup, 2000.

Apache: Inside the Cockpit of the World's Most Deadly Fighting Machine by Ed Macy, 2008.

Prehospital Emergency Care by Joseph J. Mistovich, Keith J. Karren, Howard A. Werman, and Brent Q. Hafen., 2010.

films and videos

The Surge: The Whole Story, directed by Bruce Van Dusen, 2009.

Apache Warrior, directed by David Salzberg and Christian Tureaud, 2017.

ABOUT THE AUTHOR

Vince Guerra lives in Wasilla, Alaska. His writing can be found at vinceguerra.com and Ricochet.com. *The Stars and Their Places* is his second book, the latest in a four-book series that started with *Beyond The Golden Hour.* His third book, *Pegasus,* is scheduled for release in 2020.

Subscribe via email at vinceguerra.com/allies to receive news and updates on these and other projects in production.

Also by Vince Guerra

The Golden Hour: The hour immediately following traumatic injury in which medical treatment to prevent irreversible internal damage and optimize the chance of survival is most effective.

SEAL team Polaris is on a reconnaissance mission high in the Hindu Kush mountains of Afghanistan when they're led into an ambush. The A-10 fighter providing close-air support is shot down and Air Force pararescue jumpers, dispatched to extract the downed pilot, also suffer heavy fire

As the clock ticks and casualties mount, the PJs join forces with Polaris – facing subzero temperatures, formidable terrain, and entrenched enemies – to rescue the missing pilot and get them all home.

"The violence erupts with extraordinary narrative force. ...a grippingly realistic rendering of military combat...A richly synoptic peek into a military operation." – Kirkus Reviews